"*My baby...*"

All her protests had been futile. Rafe had known all along she was pregnant.

"So, Jennifer...you and I are going to be parents in a little under six months. We're practically strangers, we've hardly spoken and barely touched, let alone made love, but we've engaged in the most intimate act two human beings can share...the procreation of life."

She blushed. "That was a medical procedure. You had nothing to do with it!"

Rafe's hand crept under the band of her jumper, and found the silky skin of her belly.

She jumped. "What are you doing?"

"I just want to see if I can feel my baby...."

DO NOT
Disturb

Anything can happen behind closed doors!

Do you dare find out...?

Some of your favorite Harlequin Presents® authors
are exploring this delicious fantasy in our sizzling,
sensual miniseries DO NOT DISTURB!

Circumstances throw different couples together in a
whirlwind of unexpected attraction. Forced into each
other's company whether they like it or not, they're
soon in the grip of passion—and definitely *don't*
want to be disturbed!

Coming next month:

The Bedroom Incident
by
Elizabeth Oldfield
Harlequin Presents #1994

SUSAN NAPIER

Honeymoon Baby

DO NOT Disturb

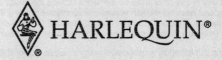

HARLEQUIN®

TORONTO • NEW YORK • LONDON
AMSTERDAM • PARIS • SYDNEY • HAMBURG
STOCKHOLM • ATHENS • TOKYO • MILAN • MADRID
PRAGUE • WARSAW • BUDAPEST • AUCKLAND

ISBN 0-373-11985-2

HONEYMOON BABY

First North American Publication 1998.

CHAPTER ONE

JENNIFER was filling a vase at the kitchen sink when the sleek, low-slung dark green car came gunning around the tree-lined curve of the driveway, almost fish-tailing into a bank of ferns as the driver belatedly realised the bend was a lot sharper than it looked. She frowned out of the window as she watched the unfamiliar car recover from its near-skid and continue at a more cautious pace up the narrow, rutted gravel drive to park in front of the low dry-stone wall which enclosed the cottage garden in front of the house. With the heavy dust coating the tinted windscreen she couldn't make out the driver, but the lone pair of skis strapped to the moulded black roof-rack suggested a stray single hoping for a bed.

Whoever it was would be out of luck. Jennifer disliked having to turn custom away, but all her rooms were currently occupied and—she unconsciously crossed her fingers—apart from a few odd days, booking was fairly solid for the rest of the month…providing the mountain minded its manners.

She glanced out of the corner window at the billowing, dirty grey mushroom-cloud of steam and ash which boiled up from the snowy summit of Mount Ruapehu, blotting out the formerly blue sky. The scenery was spectacular but living on the borders of a National Park, within twenty kilometres of an active volcano, had its drawbacks. Although there had been no major eruption here for thousands of years, the 2797-metre-high mountain itself was a powerful reminder of man's vulnerability to the forces of nature, and lately a series of minor

eruptions had put a serious crimp in the local economy
of one of New Zealand's premier ski resorts.

Jennifer's wide mouth turned down at the corners
at the thought of another disappointing winter.
Vulcanologists and government scientists had been
closely monitoring the mountain since it had exploded
back into life just over a year ago, coating the ski fields
with successive layers of brown ash for months, causing
the closure of the mountain to skiers, sightseers and
climbers, and creating great financial hardship for the
local businesses who were heavily reliant on a good ski
season for the greater portion of their annual income.
There had been no loss of life or property, but the dam-
age in terms of adverse publicity had been considerable.

Now, just as the public alert level had finally been
dropped and early snowfalls presaged a long ski season
that would enable the local tourist industry to recoup
some of the previous year's losses, Mount Ruapehu was
rumbling again, sending steam and sediment from its
crater lake streaming into the atmosphere. Although the
scientists claimed there was no indication that the new
eruption would be any bigger than last year's, casual
skiers were already cancelling their holidays in droves.
Only the hard-core snow-junkies seemed willing to gamble on parts of the ski fields remaining open for the
duration of their stay.

Fortunately a small, quiet bed and breakfast establish-
ment like Beech House appealed more to mature tourist
couples and lone travellers than to groups of avid skiers,
so Jennifer hoped to weather the crisis better than some
of the other, larger moteliers and resort operators, whose
advertising was focused on pre-packaged ski deals.
Some of her guests were even booked in *because,* rather
than in spite of the possibility of a more fiery eruption.

Jennifer's mouth curved up again, tawny brown eyes
glowing in a secret smile of contentment behind her

tortoiseshell spectacles. At least this year she didn't have to suffer the black panic of wondering whether she was going to be able to meet the next mortgage payment...

The sound of a car door opening switched her attention back to the new arrival as a slight figure glided into the kitchen to place some garden produce and a bunch of brilliant yellow chrysanthemums on the bench.

'Snazzy car. Who is it?' asked Susie Tang, going on tiptoe to peer out of the window.

Even so, her glossy black head barely came up to Jennifer's collarbone. Although five feet ten wasn't much over average height for a woman, she always felt like a veritable Amazon next to her diminutive part-time employee. 'My guess is foreign, lost or illiterate...or maybe just someone who doesn't believe "No Vacancy" signs.'

'Uh-oh!' Susie clapped her hand over her mouth, her almond-shaped eyes widening under her jet-black fringe. 'I said I'd hang it out for you when I left yesterday, didn't I? Sorry, Jen, I forgot...' The mournful mobility of her expression banished any illusion of oriental inscrutability. Susie's every thought and mood registered on her face.

A masculine hand splayed on the roof of the car as the driver hauled himself out of his bucket seat. 'Never mind—if he gets a look inside and likes what he sees, maybe he'll come back and stay another time,' said Jennifer, reaching for the flowers. A lot of her custom came from repeat business or via word-of-mouth recommendation.

'Wow!' Susie was nearly falling out of the window. 'He's even snazzier than his car! Since there's no room at the inn do you think *I* could interest him in bed and breakfast?'

Jennifer's laughing reply died in her throat as the man lifted his head in a quick, predatory motion to stare up at the house. The sun flared off hair the colour of old gold and the black wrap-around sunglasses couldn't disguise the distinctive jut of his high cheekbones and the hollow cheeks bracketing the unshaven chin. A wave of nauseating disbelief washed over her, making her knees sag against the kitchen cupboards.

Surely fate couldn't be so cruel!

She clutched the vase to her stomach, slopping water onto the tiled surface of the bench, praying that her eyes were deceiving her.

Gravel crunched under his feet as he strode around to the back of the car and opened the boot. Faded jeans moulded long legs and lean hips, and a cream woollen jumper under the black hip-length leather jacket studded with snaps and zips completed the image of threatening masculinity. He hefted a suitcase out of the boot, moving with the easy confidence of a man in the prime of his life, at the peak of his virility...

And definitely no wild illusion.

'Oh, *God*—!'

'Jen, what's the matter? You look as if you've seen a ghost?'

Worse than a ghost. Much, much worse! She was staring into the face of grim reality. A nightmare complication to an already convoluted existence. A living, breathing reproach to her unquiet conscience.

She had thought him safely ensconced in London. What hellish coincidence had landed him here, in her own private little corner of the world?

Oh, *God*!

'Jen, you're not going to pass out on me, are you? *Jen*?'

Susie's sharp anxiety penetrated her ringing skull, beating back the icy chills of disbelief which had frozen her brain. She shook her head violently, self-preservation screaming to the fore as she jerked back from the window.

'No, I'm fine,' she lied, grabbing the bunch of chrysanthemums and haphazardly stuffing them into the pottery vase.

'Is it him? That man? Do you know him?' Susie angled herself against the glass to watch him vanish around the corner of the sprawling bungalow, in the direction of the front porch. 'If he's bringing in his bag perhaps he's not just cold-calling. Maybe there's been a mix-up in the bookings. If he spoke to Paula on the phone—you know she's not big on writing things down...'

At the mention of her mother Jennifer's heart leapt in her chest. Thank goodness she wasn't here! She and Aunty Dot had driven over to The Grand Château for a Gourmet Club luncheon at the hotel restaurant; they should be away for at least another hour.

There was a welcoming bark and the loud scrabble of claws on the wooden porch, and seconds later the harsh grind of the old-fashioned doorbell reverberated in the entranceway. To Jennifer it sounded uncannily like the knell of doom.

'Uh, shouldn't you go and see what he wants?' suggested Susie when the bell rang a second time.

If the newcomer got impatient and tried the door, he would find that it wasn't locked. He could just walk in, and then, and then...

Oh, God!

'You do it,' she blurted.

'Me?'

Guests and potential guests were always dealt with by either Paula or Jennifer at their own insistence—the personal touch was a hallmark of Beech House. Susie's job was only peripheral to the bed and breakfast business—helping run Paula's afternoon cooking classes and delivering the jams, pickles and jars of edible and decorative preserved fruit, which she sold to stores as far away as Taupo.

'I have to put these flowers in the Carters' room. Mrs Carter complained that the vase of daphne that Mum put in there was too highly perfumed,' babbled Jennifer, conscious of the feebleness of her excuse.

She couldn't blame Susie for looking bewildered at her urgency over the floral arrangements. Mr and Mrs Carter had gone on a cruise on Lake Taupo for the day and wouldn't be back until late evening.

'Are you sure you're feeling all right?'

The doorbell rang again and Jennifer flinched, splashing water from the crammed vase down the leg of her fawn trousers.

'I do feel a bit sick,' she admitted bluntly, grabbing at the straw. 'Look, all you have to do is say that we don't have any vacancies for the foreseeable future, and direct him to another B&B or one of the hotels. Don't go into details. And don't give him one of our new advertising leaflets; I haven't decided how to use them yet,' she tacked on hastily, remembering the glossy reprints that her mother had ordered as a surprise, with *'Jenny Jordan and Paula Scott, proprietors'* in flowing bold type on the front.

'But, how—?'

'For goodness' sake, Susie, I'm only asking you to answer the door, not perform brain surgery!' she snapped.

Susie blinked, more surprised than offended by the implied insult. In the three months that she had worked at Beech House she had never known Jennifer be anything but kind, considerate and polite, if a little wicked in her sense of humour. Perhaps, though, a little moodiness was only to be expected from now on...

'OK, OK—don't get your hormones in a bunch.' She grinned. 'I'll go...but, uh, what if he asks—?'

'Just get rid of him!'

Jennifer bit her lip as Susie shot out of the kitchen, propelled by the low-voiced shriek. She was going to have to apologise, but later—when the immediate danger had passed and she had control of herself again.

Not wanting to compound her sins by being caught out in another lie, she forced her shaky legs into action, slipping through the dining and living rooms and sneaking out along the sweeping back verandah, leaving a faint trail in the thin mantle of volcanic ash. She let herself into the large double bedroom which was considered the best in the house for its unobscured view of Ruapehu. Closing the French doors on the icy southerly wind, she picked up the crystal vase with its artfully arranged sprays of daphne and replaced it with the flung together chrysanthemums.

She looked blankly around the room that she had tidied earlier. Should she wait in here until she heard his car leave? She eyed the door to the passage, which was slightly ajar. She longed to creep up to the sanctuary of her bedroom and bolt the door, but the narrow staircase to the converted attic was in full view of the front door.

She turned away, catching sight of her glazed expression in the old-fashioned mirror atop the dressing table. No wonder Susie had looked at her with such concern! She had never considered herself a beauty, but right now the too-square face with its too-sharp nose and slightly asymmetrical mouth was starkly plain—her dark brown hair, tumbling in careless waves to her shoulders, contrasting with a complexion as pale and waxy as the daphne blooms that she held in her hand. The bright red jumper that her mother had knitted the previous winter further accentuated her pallor, and snugly defined full breasts which trembled as if she had just run a marathon. With her left eyebrow twitching above the thin amber curve of her round spectacle frame, she looked like a woman on the verge of a nervous breakdown.

Which was exactly how she felt.

The cloying sweetness of daphne clogged her nostrils as she paced. Why on earth was Susie taking so long to get rid of him?

A vivid picture of golden male confidence sketched itself in her head and she halted on a silent moan. What if Susie couldn't handle it?

What if he chose to flex his insufferable arrogance and argue?

What if he exercised his brutal charm and insinuated himself over the threshold?

And what if his being here wasn't simply a rotten piece of malignant bad luck?

She stared out at the smouldering mountain, so busy agonising over the possibilities that she didn't notice the door to the hall swinging open until a squeak of the hinges made her stiffen.

'Playing hard to get, *Mrs Jordan*?'

Jennifer's quickened breathing hitched to an uneven stop as she slowly turned around, to be impaled by green-gold eyes which were every bit as cruelly condemning as she remembered. But now their contemptuous coldness was super-heated to a vaporous fury that made her wish he hadn't taken off his sunglasses.

Her face was on fire while her hands and feet felt like lumps of ice. Black dots prickled across her vision and her tongue suddenly felt too big for her dry mouth.

'R-Raphael. What a surprise. Wh-what are you doing here?' she managed threadily.

Raphael Jordan advanced into the spacious room, shrinking it to the size of a jail cell, his cynical smile oozing pure menace.

'What do *you* think, *Mrs Jordan*?'

She swallowed, trying to work moisture into the dry-

ness of her throat, wishing that he would stop sneering
her name in that ominously insulting fashion.

'I don't know,' she said, meaning she didn't dare
speculate. 'Are—are you just passing through on holiday?'

He bludgeoned aside the frail hope. 'Not a holiday—
a hunting expedition.' He kept on moving, forcing her
to back up until her calves hit the dressing table drawers.
'For certain very valuable—and very elusive—kiwis...'

Jennifer's stomach lurched sickeningly at his use of
the plural. 'K-kiwis are a fully protected bird,' she stut-
tered stupidly. Although she knew he was only just over
six feet, he seemed to loom for ever. 'It's against the
law for people to hunt them.'

His feral gaze gloated over her white face. 'In their
native habitat, yes, but what happens to greedy kiwis
who venture where they don't belong and violate the
laws of nature...? I'd say that makes them fair game,
wouldn't you?'

He made no attempt to touch her, yet she sensed his
straining muscles yearning to do physical violence. Her
heartbeat thundered in her ears, her eyes sliding away
from his grim expression to search the empty doorway
behind him.

'Where's Susie? What did you say to get her to let
you in?' Her cold hands were suddenly as clammy as
her brow and her voice sank to a horrified whisper.
What have you told her?

His shrug was a ripple of expensive leather. 'About
our relationship? How about the truth?'

She fought against the bile rising in her throat. 'What
truth?'

His full-lipped smile was cruelly taunting.

'Why, that you're my father's wife, pregnant with my
child!'

The heavy vase slipped through Jennifer's nerveless fingers, smashing to pieces on the polished hardwood floor as she tumbled headlong into the smothering darkness.

CHAPTER TWO

'JEN? Hello! Are you in there?'

Jennifer's eyes fluttered open to find Susie's round face filling her vision.

'Thank goodness! How do you feel?'

Jennifer moistened her dry lips, momentarily disorientated by the discovery that she was lying flat on the living room couch, with Susie kneeling on the floor beside her.

'OK...I think,' she wavered, remembering her awful anxiety dream. Had she been taking a nap? Was her guilt now going to pursue her even into sleep? 'What happened?'

'You fainted. Switched out like a light, apparently. Luckily your husband caught you before you fell face first into all that glass.'

'Husband?' she echoed feebly.

'I guess you were too busy feeling rotten to really look at our visitor, huh?' Susie suggested with a wry grin. 'I felt horribly embarrassed when I found out who I was giving the bum's rush to, but fortunately Rafe seems a forgiving kind of guy.'

'My *husband*?' Jennifer struggled up onto her elbows, her whirling head causing her to sink back against the padded arm of the couch. '*Rafe?*'

'Yeah—he said not to worry about it, that he knew you weren't expecting him. He wanted to surprise you, but I suppose it wasn't such a hot idea when you were feeling so wonky...'

So it hadn't been a dream!

'He's really here?' Jennifer cast a hunted look around

15

the room, her eyes skipping over the comfortable, well-used furniture. Everything was still fuzzy around the edges. She groped at her face.

'My glasses—where are my glasses?' She needed a barrier, however flimsy and transparent, to hide behind.

Susie picked them up off the coffee table and handed them to her to fumble on.

'Now, don't fret,' she said, misunderstanding Jennifer's panic. 'He'll be back in a moment. I got him to carry you out here because your clothes got splashed and I knew you wouldn't want the Carters' bedclothes all damp when you'd just made all the beds. He's just in the kitchen getting you a drink. See, here he is back!'

Susie scrambled to her feet to allow the tall, whipcord-lean man to weave around the coffee table and perch sideways on the broad couch. He wedged his right hip against Jennifer's side as he braced one arm on the cushioned back and leaned over to offer her a sip from the glass of water in his other hand, effectively caging in her body with his chest.

Satisfied that her employer was in good hands, Susie backed away. 'I'm going to leave for home before this volcanic fog gets any worse, but don't worry about that mess in the Carters' room, Jen, I'll clean it up for you before I go. That way you two can just concentrate on each other...'

'Thanks, Susie.' Rafe's deep, warm tone cut off Jennifer's spluttering objection as he pressed the glass to her pale mouth. He threw a burnished smile over his shoulder. 'You're a sweetheart, but...' He trailed off, raising silky brows.

Susie laughed, as if she had known him for years rather than merely minutes. 'I know, I know—three's a crowd. I guess I'll see you later then...much later!'

Jennifer pushed at the glass which had been used to

gag her as Susie scampered away. 'Take it away! I don't want a drink.'

Trust Jordan to have suborned her ally while she was unconscious. As a former male model, and former editor of a raunchy men's magazine, he was no doubt used to women falling over themselves to be friendly.

There was no smile for her. Just a probing look. 'Too bad. You need extra fluids to counteract shock—and don't tell me you're not shocked to see me. Drink!'

The glass clinked against her resistant teeth, forcing her head back against the arm of the couch, and, knowing his stubbornness, she took a single swallow, defiantly tiny.

'Again,' he insisted.

Another, even tinier sip. 'Bully,' she muttered, wondering if she dared spit it in his face.

'Cheat. Gold-digger,' he retaliated softly. *'Thief.'*

At the heavy significance placed on the last insult she almost choked on the small mouthful, the blood surging up into her face.

'Good. You've got a little of your colour back,' he said, studying her clinically. The simmering violence with which he had confronted her in the bedroom was gone, superceded by an implacable air of purpose that was even more threatening. He had taken advantage of her unconsciousness to firmly establish himself in her household, leaving her no option but to fight a rear-guard action.

Close up, his lightly tanned face revealed the imprint of thirty-three years rich with experience, fine lines fanning out from the corners of his knowing eyes and cynical curves bracketing the corners of his sensual mouth. The slight stubble softening the hard line of his jaw sparkled like gold glitter on a Christmas card, and the short, spiky tufts of deep blonde hair, sun-bleached almost white at the tips, created an improbable halo above the narrow temples. However, apart from his name, any similarity to an angel was purely illusory—no angel possessed Raphael Jordan's decadent past!

'More?'

He tilted the glass, ignoring her sullen resistance, and a trickle of water repelled by the compressed seam of her lips skated down from the corner of her mouth.

To her intense shock Rafe bent his head and licked the droplets off her chin before they could drip into the cowl-neck of her angora jumper.

'Stop it!' she gasped, wiping the back of her hand over the spot where his moist tongue had lashed her tender skin with fire. 'What do you think you're doing?'

She gulped as he lifted his head, just enough for her to see the sexual taunting in his emerald eyes.

'Just my husbandly duty, *Mrs Jordan*...'

She hated the ease with which he could disrupt her senses. From the first time Sebastian had introduced her to his son she had been deeply aware of the dangerous undercurrents, and was secretly grateful for the strained relationship between the two men which had kept their association to a minimum.

'You said you told Susie the truth,' she said, her voice ragged with the effort of controlling her fear.

He placed the barely touched glass on the beechwood coffee table without releasing her from his tormenting gaze. 'Actually, she didn't give me the chance,' he admitted with a cool lack of remorse for the fright he had given her. 'I told her my name and before I could say that I was looking for my father's wife—'

'His *widow*!' It was a distinction that was vital to Jennifer's bruised sensibilities.

He inclined his head, his eyes glinting as if her fierce correction had accorded him some kind of important victory.

'Whatever... As soon as I said I was Raphael Jordan,

she began talking as if *I* was your husband. She seemed so certain that your husband's name was Rafe, and so positive that you'd be over the moon to see me that I thought it best not to argue with her romantic delusions.'

Best? He meant most useful to his own purposes!

Jennifer clenched her hands at her sides, hating the helplessness of her position but knowing she would be no match for Rafe in a physical tussle. He clearly had no intention of letting her up until she was intimidated into giving him some answers.

She would have to rely on her wits to extricate herself and somehow persuade him to leave before he encountered loose-tongued Susie again, or—God forbid—her mother!

'It seems funny that she should get so mixed up,' he mused perilously, 'because she seemed otherwise a fairly intelligent and switched-on young woman. Could it be, dear stepmama, that you've been purposely vague about the whereabouts of your husband? Haven't you let on that he's no longer in the land of the living? Been keeping your widow's mite secret from your impecunious friends and relatives?'

Her stomach roiled at his clever guess. But not clever enough!

'Don't call me that! And how can you be so flippant about the death of your own father? I know you two didn't get on, but you might at least have some respect for his memory—'

'If you'd bothered to hang around for the funeral you would have seen me paying my respects,' he ripped at her. 'I even shed a few tears for the stiff-necked old bastard. But don't expect me to elevate him to sainthood just because he's dead. He was a good doctor and a brilliant businessman, but he was a poor husband and a rotten father; his ambitions always got in the way of his relationships and he never stopped trying to force me

into his own mould. So don't preach to me about my
filial duty, Stepmama—'

Worms of horror squirmed across her skin. 'Stop *calling* me that!'

'Why, isn't that what you became when you married
my father?'

'Because it's—it's…'

His eyes followed the inarticulate workings of her
crooked mouth.

'Ridiculous? Distasteful?' A lethal pause before he
leaned forward and added insinuatingly, *'Obscene?'*

He was close, too frighteningly close. She steadied
herself and got her tongue to shape her choppy breath
into a crisp, 'Definitely ridiculous.'

'But technically correct. And Sebastian was always
big on getting the technicalities right, wasn't he? That's
how he was able to create such a truly unique inheritance
for us to share…'

She could feel the warmth of his breath swirling
around her face, causing the blood to sing in her cheeks.
Hadn't she read somewhere about a predator which
breathed on its trapped prey before tearing it to pieces?
The animal version of a ritual act of gloating possession…

'I didn't expect Sebastian to leave me anything in his
will—he told me he wouldn't,' she said, in the desperate
hope that he was referring to the money. She silently
cursed Sebastian for breaking his promise. His God complex at work again. Even from the grave he couldn't
resist trying to get his own way! If he had stuck to their
original agreement there would have been no reason for
anyone from the Jordan family to search her out.

'I don't want to cheat anyone in the family out of
their inheritance,' she told him, her light brown eyes
owlishly earnest behind the little round spectacles.
'When Sebastian's lawyers wrote to tell me about the

shares and bonds, I wrote back and said I didn't want
them, that I'd sign a waiver of claim so they could be
returned to the estate—'

His crack of cynical laughter cut her off.

'Sure, why bother with the petty change when you've
already got your hot little hands on the main prize,
right?' he growled, abruptly dropping his arm from the
back of the couch and planting his hands on the arm of
the couch, on either side of her head.

'I—I don't know what you mean,' she said warily,
excruciatingly aware of his thumb-tips brushing the
straining cords of her neck and the metal zip of his open
jacket sawing at the soft wool over her breasts as the
heavy sides enfolded her like black leather wings.

'No? Apart from all the hard cash you gouged out of
him while he was alive, under the terms of the Jordan
family trust, as my father's legal wife at the time of his
death you've inherited his position as trustee of a multi-
million-dollar investment fund! I notice you're not offering to waive *that* family privilege!'

She bit her pale lower lip. 'That's only a nominal
title—the trust is still going to be run by the three professional trustees, exactly as it was when Sebastian was
alive. And if you're familiar with the deed then you must
know that as a named trustee I have no legal access to
any of that money.'

'Not for yourself personally, I agree,' he said silkily,
'but any *child* conceived during your marriage to
Sebastian would be a blank cheque in your hands...'

'No...! Never!'

Her appalled cry of rejection was followed by a short,
electric silence.

Jennifer felt the hairs rise on the back of her neck and
a metallic taste flood her tongue. How could he have
found out? she thought hysterically. Sebastian had as-
sured her that his exclusive London clinic guaranteed

total confidentiality and that his staff were well trained
in protecting the anonymity of both donor and recipient.
Ethics had obliged him to hand over her case to one of
his senior colleagues, and Sebastian's rapidly failing
health had meant he rarely visited the clinic himself, but
he had promised to sequester her case-notes amongst his
own inactive files as an extra precaution.

Of course, those staunch ethics of his—which had
been so vital to her trust—had in the end turned out to
be tainted by self-interest. Maybe he had been unforgive-
ably lax in other ways, too... Or maybe Raphael was
just making guesses based more on his cynical certainty
that Jennifer was a greedy bimbo out for everything she
could get than any real hard evidence.

Her hands instinctively crept to protect her flat ab-
domen.

Rafe's eyes flickered down as he registered the movement and returned to hers, gleaming with yellow fire.

'Scruples, Jennifer? From a woman who married a
dying old man for his money?'

He was making it all sound so *sordid,* when in fact it
had been an eminently practical arrangement on both
sides.

'It wasn't *like* that—'

'You're not trying to claim it was *love*?' The word
was uttered with a deep contempt that seemed to sum
up Raphael Jordan's views on relationships in general,
and Jennifer in particular.

She flushed and tried to cling to her fast-dwindling
courage. She recognised his interrogation technique. He
was harrying her in ever-decreasing circles, slipping under her defences to nip painfully at his target and then
retreating to prowl around another topic before darting
in for another bite.

Somewhere in the background she heard Susie carol
out a goodbye, and the front door bang, and a little of

her tension eased. At least now if there was a messy scene there would be no witnesses.

She would have liked to fling Raphael's cynicism back in his teeth with a passionate declaration of emotion, but instead chose the dignity of the literal truth. 'I liked Sebastian from the time I first met him. I had a lot of respect for him—'

She broke off, for that respect had taken a severe beating the day he died...

'And I'll bet you liked him a whole lot more when you discovered he had inoperable cancer, hmm?' said Rafe crudely. 'He told you about it, didn't he? When he was staying here?'

'Yes, but—'

'So—out of pure altruism, of course—you instantly agreed to abandon your home and business and travel back to England with Sebastian as his—now how did he introduce you to the family?—ah, that's right, his *"nurse-companion"*...the one with a murky past and no credentials!'

A sunburst of anger overrode Jennifer's guilt. She still vividly remembered the humiliation she had suffered at the hands of three of Sebastian's bickering ex-wives and his numerous, spoiled, grown-up stepchildren when they realised that an Antipodean nobody was threatening their future access to the Jordan gravy-train.

Only Raphael, Sebastian's eldest son and sole natural child, had remained aloof from the outpourings of spite which followed. Never having allowed his father to bankroll his lifestyle, he was immune to the bribes and rewards by which Sebastian had manipulated his greedy brood of dependents-by-marriage. Although Rafe had bluntly disapproved of his father's precipitous marriage to a woman thirty-six years his junior, in keeping with his own history of rebellious independence he had not disputed Sebastian's right to make a bloody fool of himself.

'I *did* train as a nurse—I just never got to complete the practical part of the course for my formal qualification,' she flared now.

'Yes, well, you were obviously better qualified as a *companion* than a nurse, because lo and behold, only a month after you land in England you're married to your patient—and three weeks after *that* your very wealthy new husband, whose heart was never a contributor to his health problems, has a heart attack in his own bed and is dead within days. And what does his doting bride do to mourn his passing? She skips out on the funeral, leaving only a post office box on the other side of the world as a forwarding address...'

Jennifer gasped. 'If you're trying to imply that I had *any*thing at all to do with Sebastian having heart failure—!'

'Oh, no, I've read the autopsy report and spoken to his doctors...I have to absolve you of murder,' he conceded, with what she thought was insulting reluctance.

'Kind of you!' she snapped recklessly.

He raised silky eyebrows. 'It does happen: energetic, lusty young wife entices her elderly, ailing husband to prove that he's still a man...'

Her tawny eyes flashed up at him, her fingers itching to slap his face, but before she could act out the impulse his eyelids drooped and he purred, 'Only we both know how unlikely *that* scenario is...since my father's cancer treatments had made him impotent well before he ever left on that round-the-world trip. Your marriage was never actually consummated, was it, Jennifer—?'

Her fingers curled into her palms. 'You have no right to—'

'I saw his medical records after he died...I *know* that

claim of paternity you got him to sign isn't worth the paper it's written on!'

'I don't know what you're talking about—'

'I'm talking about the "bargain" you made with Sebastian, the one that you're going to use to unlock the trust.'

She clapped her hands over her ears. 'I refuse to listen to—'

His strong fingers wrapped around her wrists, wrenching them away from her head. He pinned them against the centre of his chest with one hand and used the other to cup her chin, forcing her to acknowledge what he was saying.

'Oh, no, you're not getting out of it that easily. If you won't tell this story, then *I* will—and you're going to listen to every single, solitary word!'

While his eyes, feasting on her every reaction, were no doubt going to be her judge, jury and executioner! Jennifer tried to congeal her expressive features into a stony mask.

'It's one of life's little ironies that my father the fertility specialist discovered not long after his divorce from my mother that he'd become sterile himself,' Rafe said harshly. 'But typically he never reconciled himself to it. Practically from the time I hit puberty he was nagging at me to find a steady girlfriend. As far as he was concerned my sole purpose in life was to become a doctor like him and marry early so that I could have lots of little Jordan brats. When I told him I didn't intend to do any of those things—ever—he began taking wives with children of their own, and when that proved unsatisfactory he started throwing genetically desirable women in my path, offering bribes to the first one to get pregnant and to the altar.'

His voice hummed with remembered fury, his pupils smouldering coals ringed with green fire. Ignoring the curiosity that was eating away at her outrage, Jennifer pushed ineffectually against his thick cabled sweater as she tried to twist her wrists out of his unyielding grasp. He responded by adjusting his grip on her chin, his long thumb sliding under the point of her jaw to dig into the soft flesh and find her furious pulse.

'Finally, last year, I figured out the perfect way to get him off my back. I went to his clinic's IVF sperm bank and made a generous donation to his fertility pro-gramme. Afterwards I told him that now he could popu-late the whole damned world with his precious genes— I was out of the loop!'

Jennifer's struggles were momentarily eclipsed by a wickedly inappropriate desire to laugh. Sebastian's tell-ing had differed greatly from Rafe's, and no wonder! Sebastian had regarded his work with an almost religious seriousness, and his son's act of cheeky irreverence must have been a grave offence to his pride.

'Funnily enough, he was furious at what I'd done,' confirmed Rafe sardonically. 'It turned out that mere ge-netic reproduction wasn't his aim, it was the *family* con-nection that was the vital requirement—another legiti-mate Jordan heir to perpetuate the name along with the genes. Then his cancer was diagnosed and he suddenly seemed to lose interest in the idea.

'I should have known better than to think he'd given up his pet obsession. He just went off on his annual world trip and did what he'd done so often in the past— he bought himself what he wanted. He bought himself a wife: a strong, fertile, healthy woman who would pan-der to his sick fantasies and allow him to father his own grandchild—'

'*No!*' Jennifer began to struggle again, kicking out helplessly with her legs as she squirmed in his hold.

'He paid you to undergo artificial insemination at his

clinic, in a new IVF procedure with a high rate of success: my sperm injected directly into your egg—'

'*No!*'

'—and re-implanted in your body. Of course, this all happened in the weeks before your wedding, because there was no point in him marrying you until you had been confirmed with a viable pregnancy.'

'You're mad!' she panted. 'I don't know where you get your *bizarre* ideas from but you know what you can do with them. I'm *not* pregnant.'

He had to believe her. He *had* to!

'No?' He let go her captive hands, sliding his palm down to rest firmly on her lower belly.

'No!'

She blinked defiantly back at him, confident that there wasn't even the hint of a swell under her waistband. Against her silence he could prove nothing. *Nothing!*

He splayed his fingers and applied a light pressure, just enough to make her aware of the heat of his hand seeping through the damp-splashed woollen fabric.

'Do you always faint like that—at the drop of a hat?' he asked, his thumb discovering the front placket that concealed her zip.

'It wasn't a hat you dropped, it was a bombshell,' she pointed out. 'An ox would have fainted!'

He smiled, that full-lipped smile of bitter scepticism. 'Aren't you even going to ask me how I know all the gory details?'

'Since there are no details to know, gory or otherwise, I'm not in the least interested in your speculations,' she bluffed wildly, jerking her chin from his hand. 'I think *you're* the one who has been having the sick fantasies.'

For some reason he seemed to find that genuinely amusing. 'You could be right.'

She pounced on the faint lightening of his mood. 'So,

would you mind letting me up? I can't lie around here all day. I have work to do.'

His smile faded. 'Actually, I do mind. I still haven't finished my examination.' His thumbnail tauntingly flipped the tiny metal tab of her zip and her hand slapped down over his.

'Don't you dare!'

It was the wrong thing to say to a man who lived life strictly on his own terms, and who, according to his disgruntled father, cared nothing for history or tradition or polite behaviour. A man who flaunted his vices before the world without the least consideration for the embarrassment he had caused his family.

He gave the tab a sharp little downward tug, and when Jennifer screeched and clutched at her gaping zip with both hands he swiftly transferred his attention to her heaving breasts, cupping and lifting them for his bold appraisal.

'Is it just my imagination, or are these a bit more lush than they were three months ago?' he baited her, fluffing the red angora with his swirling fingertips as he traced her generous contours. 'Mmm, I certainly don't remember them being a D-cup, and there are plenty of people who can testify that I'm an infallible judge of a woman's breast size...'

He also was the most despicable man she had ever met!

Jennifer yanked up her zip with shaking fingers, hunching her shoulders to try and evade his provocative touch. 'You, you—'

'Oh, yes, definitely bigger,' he decided, cuddling the firm mounds together so that they were plumped into even greater prominence. 'I understand pregnancy makes them more sensitive, too...' He rubbed his thumbs goadingly across the soft tips, and to her horror Jennifer felt them tingle and begin to push against the lace constriction of her bra. In a few moments he would be able to feel her treacherous response for himself.

Shame and fear exploded the last of her caution. She slapped his mocking face, hard, his gold whiskers rasping like sandpaper against her furious palm.

'Take your hands off me! How many times do I have to say it? *I am not pregnant!*' she shrieked at him. 'I'm *nothing*. Can't you get that through your thick head? Yes, I was your father's wife for a very brief time but now he's gone and it's *over*. It's *history*. I came back here because this is my *home*. This is where I want to live my life. I don't care what you *think* you know about me, unlike you and your paranoid family of snobs, I don't happen to enjoy living in a world where everyone is judged by how they dress and what they own rather than who they are and what they've achieved. I *told* you I won't interfere with the estate, so why can't you just go back to where you came from and *leave me alone*?'

His blond-tipped head had snapped to the side, his cheek scorched by the outline of her angry fingers, and now he slowly turned back, working his jaw cautiously to and fro in his hand.

At least he had stopped touching her. Jennifer pushed herself up on stiff arms, scooting backwards with her hips so that she was half sitting, no longer helplessly submissive to his will. She had never struck anyone in anger before, and was miserably conscious that this man was responsible for a number of unfortunate firsts in her life. An apology was edging forward on her tongue when she caught sight of the punishing expression in his eyes.

'So, you're saying that my father couldn't even be honest with me on his deathbed? That the last words he ever said to me in this world were an ugly, pointless lie?'

Her blow had been a butterfly kiss in comparison.

Jennifer felt as if she had been hit on the head with a brick.

'Your father?' she croaked, devastated by this latest betrayal. If she hadn't been already sitting she would have keeled over again. 'I— I don't believe you... *Sebastian* told you those things?'

'In hospital on the night he died. The night *you* did your moonlight flit.'

She winced at his clipped contempt, utterly incapable of defending herself. There was no denying the fact that when she had angrily fled the hospital that afternoon she had made herself deliberately inaccessible. And later, when she had phoned the hospital and learned that Sebastian had died...well, she had been extremely distressed, confused and frightened—because she had still felt so angry with him for abusing her trust. Running away from an untenable situation had seemed the best and safest option.

'He deteriorated suddenly and became agitated and disorientated. He kept saying your name, but no one could find you or knew where you'd gone, and by the time I got to the hospital he was in a bad way,' said Rafe, making no attempt to spare her the brutal details. 'He was pretty heavily sedated but he knew what was going to happen, and I guess he realised it was his last chance to clear his conscience—so it all spilled out, how you had leapt at his cash-for-a-kid deal.

'He kept asking me to forgive him as he drifted in and out of consciousness, kept saying that he'd made a bad misjudgement about you, that he was worried about what you might do, what might happen to the baby if he wasn't around to protect it, babbling about betrayal and blackmail...'

'And you *believed* him?' she forced herself to say steadily. 'You didn't think it might have just been the wanderings of a drugged mind?'

'Yes. That's why I checked to see whether you'd ever been treated at the clinic.'

Her heart clenched. 'There's no way you could have had legal access to that kind of information—'

His smile mocked her naïveté. 'Who said my access was legal?'

'You—'

'Legal or not, I know to the exact minute how and when our baby was conceived.'

'*My* baby—'

The cry was out before she realised it, never to be taken back. All her protests, all her stonewalling had been futile. He had known all along and he had enjoyed watching her twist and turn until she had tangled herself up in her web of lies and evasions and more lies. She felt sick, but also oddly liberated.

'So, Jennifer…you and I are going to be parents in a little under six months.' He stroked his faintly marked cheek, and then touched hers with a gentleness that was far more blood-curdling than his former aggression. 'We're practically strangers, we've hardly spoken and barely touched, let alone made love, but we've engaged in the most intimate act two human beings can share… the procreation of life.'

His knuckles touched her chin and then ran down the centre of her jumper between her breasts, dissolving away one or two faint pearls of vase-water still nestling amongst the strands of wool, gliding down to stop in the folds at her waist. This time she made no effort to stop him, so stunned was she by his lyrically soft words. It almost sounded as if…

She shivered. 'We haven't *shared* anything—'

'I beg to differ. My seed is growing in your womb. I'd say that made us pretty damned intimate, wouldn't you?'

She blushed. 'That was a medical procedure. You had nothing to do with it.'

He laughed, and for once she couldn't detect a single cynical note in his amusement. 'I had everything to do with it—me and my little jar and my wicked stock of fantasies.'

Her blush deepened, her hands fisting on her thighs. 'You know what I mean.'

He sobered. 'Yes, I know exactly what you mean. And you're wrong. I may not have been a partner in the highly questionable deal you and my father struck but I *am* involved. You're a rich, pregnant widow because of *me*. If I'd thought about it at all I presumed that my sperm would go to help happily married infertile couples have the children they desperately wanted…not to a selfish, egotistical old man and a soon-to-be-widowed wife with extremely questionable values. As I see it, I have a responsibility here.'

'Responsibility?' Jennifer echoed, her eyes widening in horror.

'To my father—may God have taken pity on his manipulating soul—and to you.'

'But you don't have to feel responsible for me. I don't want you to!'

'And of course to my son or daughter,' he said calmly, as if she hadn't spoken. 'I suppose it's too early to tell which?'

She nodded her head dumbly. 'You can't—you told your father that you never wanted brats of your own,' she accused shrilly.

'But you and Sebastian took that decision out of my hands. Instead of giving my gift of life to some anonymous couple, Sebastian took it for himself, and in asking me to forgive him for it—the first time I've ever heard him admit he was wrong about *any*thing—he was trusting me to repair the harm he might have done. I'd be a despicable bastard if I turned my back and ignored his dying wish.'

'But I *want* you to turn your back!' she wailed. He was tormenting her again, that's all, she told herself. He was just saying those things to wind her up. He just wanted to make sure she wasn't going to try and hold the family to ransom over child support. 'I told you, I don't need anything. I'll even sign a paper saying so, if that's what you want!'

'You're very emotional, aren't you? I never noticed that when you were in London. You always seemed very quiet and practical, very restrained...a colonial country mouse in the big city. So maybe all the extra hormones flooding your system are making you touchy.'

His hand had crept under the band of her jumper while he was talking, and found the silky skin of her belly.

She jumped. 'What are you doing?'

'I just want to see if I can feel my baby.' He pushed up the band a little way, so they could both see his tanned hand contrasted against the white skin of her stomach.

His use of the word 'my' made her nervous. 'Well, you can't—even I can't feel anything yet. Stop it. I don't like you touching me.' She wished it were true. The pads of his fingers were surprisingly soft, while his palm was faintly dry and abrasive. Just below the cuff of his jacket she could see silky threads of dark blond hair dusting the back of his wrist.

'You're very pale here,' he murmured, his thick lashes masking the glitter of his curiosity. 'Don't you wear a bikini in the summer?'

'No.' He was running his finger around and around the rim of her navel, making her skin feel too tight for her body. 'Do you mind? You're making me queasy.'

He stilled the movement, but left his hand where it

was. 'Have you been having morning sickness?' he asked, studying her flushed face.

'No, I've been as healthy as a horse,' she said. 'Another reason why you're not needed.'

'Well, we'll wait and see, shall we?' He began to withdraw his hand, and whether by accident or design his middle finger slid into the indentation he had been lazily circling.

Jennifer sucked in her breath and his finger snugly rode the sudden movement of her diaphragm.

'Perfect fit,' he murmured wickedly, glancing down, then up again, catching the streak of sinful speculation in her startled gaze.

His lids drooped as he slowly withdrew his finger, and to Jennifer the whole world seemed to darken and shiver in awareness.

She knew then that the devil had green eyes and an English drawl. How else could he offer so much temptation with so little effort?

'What did you mean, wait and see?' she asked belatedly.

'Why, you don't think I came all this way just to turn around and go home again, do you?' he said, pulling her jumper back down over the top of her trousers. 'I think I need to know a great deal more about the mother of my baby before I make any decision about whether to trust her with the raising of our child. And what better place to plumb the depths of her character than in her own home?'

Her jaw dropped. 'You can't mean you intend to stay in New Zealand!'

'Not just New Zealand. Here. In this house. With you. I'm sure you could put me up for a few days, or however long it takes. You could put me in the room my father had...'

However long it takes?

Just as Jennifer was about to shoot him down in flames she heard the sound of the front door opening and two female voices mingling with excited barking, one rising to a familiar contralto lilt.

'Hello, Jenny darling, we're home! What a nightmare, I hope you've got the kettle on...'

'It's my mother! Oh, God—' Jennifer clutched at Rafe's jacket.

'Good. I'm looking forward to meeting her.'

'You can't!' She looked around, wondering frantically where to hide him. He was too big to stuff under the furniture. 'You can't let her see you.'

'I think it's too late for that,' said Rafe, rising politely to his feet as a stocky grey-haired woman in a baggy beige suit marched into the room, followed by a slender, bird-like woman in a wheelchair, whose thin face lit up at the sight of the hovering man.

'*Rafe!* How wonderful that you could come! Oh, Jenny darling, why didn't you tell me—or did he surprise you, too?' Paula Scott didn't seem to notice Rafe's dazed expression as she coasted forward to hold out her delicate hands. 'Oh, come down here, you wonderful man, and give me a kiss. I can't tell you how pleased I am to meet my daughter's husband at long last—I was beginning to think you didn't exist!'

CHAPTER THREE

JENNIFER sat tensely upright on the soft couch, balancing her cup of tea on her lap while Raphael sprawled comfortably beside her, his jacket discarded, his long legs tucked under the coffee table and his arm extended along the back of the couch so that his fingers could idly play amongst the tousled waves at the nape of her stiff neck.

'Yes, I flew into Auckland yesterday, shortly before they closed the airport because of the spreading volcanic smog,' he was telling her mother. 'I had been going to catch a connecting flight here, but when the airline said it had no idea when any of the local airports might be reopened I decided to hire a car and drive down. And I'm glad I did—it gave me a chance to see something of your wonderful countryside.'

He was certainly turning on the friendly charm, thought Jennifer sourly, brushing at the faint damp patches which still lingered on her trousers.

After being briefly disconcerted by Paula Scott's words of welcome, Rafe had quickly summed up the situation and deftly turned the scenario to his advantage. And her mother had fallen for him like a ton of bricks, leaning forward in her wheelchair, her blue eyes sparkling with animation, as Rafe described his drive and his dramatic first view of the rumbling mountain with its ash column rising thousands of feet in the air, casually comparing it with some of the world's other active volcanoes which he had witnessed in action.

Even Aunty Dot, an eccentric elderly spinster who generally treated all males with brusque impatience—being of the opinion that there were no 'real men' left in the world—was looking at him with grudging interest. An amateur naturalist and inveterate shoestring traveller, Dot was a semi-permanent resident of Beech House, living there between her long trips abroad, and anyone who brought news of fresh vistas for her to explore would be welcome grist to her mill.

'Well, thank goodness you came when you did! That was what I wanted to tell you when I came in, Jenny,' said Paula excitedly. 'We just heard on the car radio that they've upgraded the volcano alert level to three. That's on a scale of five, and it means they're classing it as a hazardous local eruption,' she explained in an aside to Rafe, before switching her attention back to her daughter.

'They've closed the mountain completely, and with the ash cloud blowing this way they're issuing a general warning for residents not to go outside without masks and to stay off the roads unless absolutely essential. Driving conditions are awful on the main road already, aren't they, Dot? We had to crawl along and the headlights didn't seem to help at all. Did you feel that earth tremor just as we arrived? That must have been another massive ash blast going up!'

Earth tremor? Taking a sip of her untasted tea, Jennifer instinctively glanced at Raphael and found him looking back, a knowing quirk at the corner of his mouth. He knew that neither of them had been aware of any external shocks. She remembered that moment of shattering temptation. A volcano had been erupting outside her window and she had still assumed it was *Rafe* who had made her world shudder!

Her cup rattled in her saucer as she replaced it with a trembling hand.

'Careful, darling,' said Rafe, leaning over to still the teetering crockery. He had already drunk half of his own tea, *and* eaten two of her mother's feather-light scones while inveigling his way into her good graces.

Jennifer's eyes told him she would like to dump the contents of her cup over his head. She wasn't fooled by his amiable air of relaxation. He knew now why Susie had made her apparently inexplicable mistake and had accepted his assigned role as her husband purely for some nefarious purpose of his own as smoothly as if he had planned it for himself.

He was relishing seeing her hoist by her own petard, knowing that he now had her precisely where he wanted her—totally at his mercy. One word and the whole elaborate charade she had created to protect her sweet, unworldly mother would come tumbling down.

If she had been the crying type she would have burst into tears. But then she doubted that even a Niagara of tears would soften Rafe's cynically hardened heart.

'I've got it, *darling*,' she responded through her beaming teeth.

'It's so lovely to see you two together,' her mother sighed, getting back on the subject that her daughter had spent the last fraught fifteen minutes trying to obscure with meaningless small talk. 'Poor Jenny has been missing you so dreadfully since she got home; she could hardly bear to talk about you—I had to base most of my impressions of you on her letters and phone calls before your marriage, and your photograph—so I hope you won't mind if I'm rudely inquisitive.'

'Of course not, Paula. If you don't mind the reverse.' Rafe's hand massaged Jenny's neck under her veil of hair, a possessive, lover-like caress that didn't go unnoticed by the two older women. 'Jenny and I didn't seem to talk about anything other than ourselves when we were together. I just hope that photo was a flattering one...' He trailed off invitingly.

As anticipated, Paula Scott glided innocently into the

trap. 'How could it not be? Having been so often in front of the camera when you were a model, I suppose it's second nature to show it your best side—not to say your other sides haven't turned out to be very attractive too,' she added, looking him over with a twinkle. 'Actually, it was your wedding photo.'

Rafe stiffened slightly, although his voice remained casually amused. 'Oh? Which one was that?'

Jennifer considered herself lucky he hadn't asked which *wedding*...

'Would you like to see?' Paula bent and felt in the tray under the seat of her wheelchair, pulling out her handbag. Her long battle against the debilitating effects of a back injury might have worn her frame thin, but not her valiant spirit. 'I hope you don't mind, Jenny—' she smiled a trifle guiltily, her gamine grin making her look more like a girl than a fifty-five-year-old woman '—but I had a copy taken off for my wallet. A mother has to have something to boast over!'

'Of course I'd love to see it,' said Rafe, with a gentle courtesy that Jennifer would have appreciated if she hadn't known he was merely sucking up for more information.

'I'm sure Rafe isn't really interested—'

'Oh, let him speak for himself, girl,' Dot chipped in, creaking heavily in her chair as she scooped another scone off the plate. 'The man has a mind of his own, doesn't he? Maybe after three months apart he needs to remind himself that he's married. I notice you don't wear a wedding ring, young man.'

Jennifer nervously fingered the heavy gold band on her left hand. 'Aunty Dot—'

'I don't believe in them, Mrs Grey,' said Rafe without turning a hair.

Dot's deep voice broke on a crack of laughter. 'Neither do I, sonny, neither do I. Never could abide a man

wearing jewellery. Namby-pamby, I call it. And you
may as well call me Dot, seeing as we're as near as
dammit related. Jenny calls me Aunty, but I'm really just
an old friend of the family.'

'A very valued friend, I'm sure, Dot.'

This time Rafe's smoothness backfired on him. 'No
need to butter me up, young man. I've already decided
you'll do. Jennifer's always had a good head on her
shoulders. If she chose you then that's good enough reason for me to like you.'

'Thank you,' Rafe chuckled, proving that unlike his
father he had no problems admitting his own faults. 'I
suppose a backhanded compliment is better than an in-
sincere one.'

'Here you are!' Jennifer's mother finally produced the
result of her rummaging in her untidy bag.

Jennifer had one more lame attempt at deflecting the
inevitable. 'He probably already has that print anyway—'

'We ex-models are terribly vain; we can never resist
drooling over shots of ourselves,' Rafe interrupted her
coolly, half rising to take the slim leather pocketbook
from Paula's deceptively fragile fingers. He settled back
beside his rigid companion and inspected the small col-
oured photograph displayed under the plastic window.

'Oh, yes, I remember that moment *very* vividly,' he
murmured, causing Jennifer to shift uneasily on the
cushions and rub her neck, which strangely seemed to
still feel his phantom fingers. She didn't have to look to
know what Rafe was seeing: a study in deception.

In deference to Sebastian's insistence that their wedding appear as normal as possible, to subvert any potential future threat to the legality of Jennifer's position, she
had worn an expensive white silk suit, paid for by
Sebastian, and had carried an exquisite bouquet of white
roses and baby's breath, and afterwards they had posed

for the register office photographer. She had been wearing her contact lenses, and a visit from a hairstylist and make-up expert had prettied her unconventional features, but it was the secret which she happily carried inside her which had made her truly bloom like a genuine bride.

To Jennifer's extreme discomfort, and Sebastian's startled satisfaction, Rafe had turned up to hear them exchange their brief vows—the only one of the extended family to attend. Although he had refused to act as a formal witness, his father had insisted on him joining them for a photograph. He had broken off one of Jennifer's white roses and thrust it through the button-hole on the lapel of his son's grey suit, lining them up with Jennifer in the middle.

In hindsight she could appreciate the irony of the pose, but at the time only Sebastian had known that the man on the other side of his wife was in fact the true father of her child. As far as Jennifer had been aware, her baby's father was irrelevant, a number on the label of an anonymous test tube of frozen sperm, chosen from hundreds of others. The anonymity was a necessary part of general fertility programmes, she had understood, to prevent genetic parents launching bids to reclaim the off-spring created from the sperm or eggs they had previously donated...or birth parents trying to sue donors for maintenance!

While in the originally posed photograph she and Rafe had been wearing identical fake smiles, a few seconds later the accidental triggering of the photographer's remote control had caught an informal shot of Sebastian nudging Jennifer into accepting Rafe's polite kiss on her cheek. Frozen on film in embarrassed mid-stumble, she had been pressing her bouquet-filled hand against Rafe's dark jacket to steady herself, and in profile it seemed as if she was looking up at him, pink-cheeked and adoring, while the three-quarter angle of his head showed clearly his smiling intent to kiss her as his arm encircled her silk-clad waist.

What *didn't* show up in the photograph was the angry pride in Jennifer's eyes and the sardonic contempt behind Rafe's teasing smile...and the gaunt, elderly groom, neatly excised from the negative she had taken to the camera shop to be reprinted.

'Jenny has a larger, framed version up in her bedroom,' said Paula fondly, wheeling over to retrieve her wallet. 'Since all our living areas are used by our guests, we like to keep our private things to ourselves.' She looked down at the photo and smiled. 'I thought this looked so lively, full of warmth and fun. It was such a relief to know that Jennifer had found someone wonderful—and for it to be Sebastian's son of all people! Your father was such a pleasant guest, so helpful and undemanding.'

Jennifer bit back a nervous giggle when she saw Rafe's eyes widen at this description of his exacting, imperious father.

'Mum always sees the best in everyone,' she said, obliquely warning him against trying to shatter her mother's rosy illusions.

'A rare and admirable quality,' Rafe murmured, looking thoughtfully from Jennifer to her mother, obviously racking up more evidence for the prosecution. 'Of course, people often act quite differently from their usual selves when they escape the pressures of their normal environment. Some of them see it as an excuse to go wild and do dangerous things that they'd never dream of doing at home...and later live to bitterly regret it.'

Jennifer knew the message was explicitly aimed at her, but as usual Paula took the words at face value.

'Oh, your father came here for the peace and quiet we could provide, not to go adventuring. But he was so very exhausted by the time he got to our section of his holiday that I was rather worried for him. Thank goodness Jenny was on hand, with her home-nursing experience, because Sebastian refused to see a doctor or alter his plans for the rest of his trip. I encouraged her, you know, to accept his offer to accompany him back to England after he said he didn't like the idea of employing a total stranger. I thought the travel would be a good chance for Jenny to broaden her mind a little—she'd never been overseas before...'

From the cynical heft of an eyebrow Jenny could see Rafe thinking that she had been plenty broad-minded by the time she had married his father.

'I was *so* sorry when she arrived back and told me that he had died,' Paula continued. 'You have my very deepest sympathy, Rafe. But at least he had the chance to see you happy first,' she added, always ready to stress the positive. 'Jenny never said, but I supposed his being in such a precarious state of health was the reason why everything happened in such a rush between the two of you...' She paused delicately.

'Thank you,' said Rafe in simple acceptance of her sympathy, warmed, as people usually were, by Paula's natural empathy. 'But the rushing part was just as much Jenny's idea. Your daughter is one determined lady once she's made up her mind about something.'

Jennifer almost choked on her tea. A lady was the last thing that he considered her to be! Coughing, she let Rafe whisk her cup and saucer out of her hands and pat her on the back with what she felt was unnecessary firmness.

'I know. She was very stubborn as a girl,' said Paula. 'And very quiet. She never seemed to need a lot of friends. Always daydreaming and scribbling and inventing her own private games with her own rules that nobody else could follow.'

'She hasn't changed much then,' said Rafe, and the tiny blade of sharpness concealed in his words made a small nick in his carefully presented image of a totally besotted husband.

'I expect you still have a lot to learn about each other,' Paula said mildly. 'It was a pity you had to dash off up the Amazon, Rafe, so soon after the wedding, and your father's death, but Jenny said that invitations to join an expedition like that are few and far between, and you had to grab the opportunity while it was offered. She said it had been a secret dream of yours for years to help the indigenous peoples of the rainforest, and she didn't want you to sacrifice it for her sake…'

Now it was Rafe's turn to choke, on nothing more than his own astounded tongue. 'The Amazon?'

'She said you'd be away at least four months, possibly six. I hope nothing went wrong that you're back early? Jenny said it could be dangerous working so far out of contact with civilisation.' Paula's head tilted in motherly concern.

'Fascinating place, the Amazon,' commented Dot, washing down the last of her scone with the dregs of her tea. 'Been there myself a few times. Marvellous specimens. Going to go back some day, I hope. Like to talk about it with you some time.'

'Uh, well, I…' It was the first time Jennifer had ever seen Raphael Jordan speechless, but unfortunately she couldn't afford to enjoy the sight of him floundering in his own witlessness.

'He just got a little unexpected R&R,' she said hurriedly. 'He had to catch all sorts of odd flights to get here, and now he has virtually to go *straight back* to be able to rejoin the team in time. *Don't you*, Rafe?'

He looked at her, her heavy-handed emphasis wiping the stunned glaze from his green eyes, replacing it with a wicked admiration that made her creamy pale cheeks

pinken. How she wished she had never embarked on this
agony of deceit!

She nervously brushed non-existent crumbs from her
lap, and her hand touched her stomach and stilled, acknowledging that she was fiercely glad her wish could
never be granted. She had what she wanted and nobody,
nobody, was going to take it away!

Rafe folded his arms over his chest, the thick cabling
on his sweater pulling tight over his shoulders, letting
his silence stretch until Jennifer was on the verge of
panic before he drawled, 'Actually, *darling*, I can take
longer if I like. Everything's been going so well we've
pretty much done what we originally set out to do...and
various members of the team are already splitting off to
take up other projects. It won't be a problem if I send a
message that I've decided not to return...'

'I thought there was no way to get communications
in or out of your area of the rainforest?' said Paula innocently.

Rafe pursed his lips to disguise his amusement.
Jennifer had thought of everything.

'Before, no—but I made special arrangements at every
step along the way on my trip out,' he replied with bland
aplomb.

'Well, that's wonderful news!' Paula beamed. 'Isn't
it, Jenny?'

Her mother's joyful exclamation was punctuated by a
low rumble and a shimmer of windows in their wooden
frames. Mount Ruapehu obviously had the same opinion
as Jennifer.

Dot got up and crossed to the glass doors, peering
towards the mountain through a fine haze of grey powder
interspersed with swirling, fingernail-sized ash flakes.

'It's pretty black up over there now,' she said.
'There's hardly a glimpse of clear sky left. I bet the

colour of that plume means most of the crater lake has gone. We could see some real pyrotechnics soon.'

She rapped at the dust-coated glass with a stubby finger. 'I hope the wind changes again, or I'm going to lose some of the plants to this damned ash. I've covered the most delicate ones, but at this time of the year they need as much sunlight as they can get.'

In spite of the fact that she travelled for about four months of every year, Dot had put herself in charge of the flower and vegetable gardens, and whenever she was in residence she worked with a passion amongst her beloved plants and planned all the new plantings. Over the years she had built up the grounds of Beech House to the point where they were regularly featured in 'open gardens' tours during local festivals.

Rafe went to join her at the window, the seams of his close-fitting jeans whitening as he stepped across Jennifer's legs, dragging her unwilling attention to his taut backside as he moved away. To her chagrin, her mother caught her looking and grinned, miming a silent whistle.

Jennifer smiled weakly in return as she began stacking the tea things on the tray. If her mother had never met her 'husband', the discreet long-distance 'divorce' that she had been planning to blame on their extended separation could have been achieved with minimum fuss. Now it would be that much more difficult.

'Are we likely to be in any danger at this distance?' she heard Rafe ask Dot.

'Not from molten material. In an eruption the size they're predicting the danger zone for that is only a few kilometres.' Geology was another of Dot's hobbies. 'But the radio said that there'd already been several big lahars through the ski fields, and once the mud-flows reach the river systems they can cause havoc downstream. There was a big train-wreck in '53, when a rail bridge over the

Whangaehu River got washed away and a hundred and fifty people were killed. But our main problem will probably just be the ash flying around and clogging things up, and then you get water shortages when people try to clean it up. And it can be toxic when it's breathed in, of course, so we'd better make sure the animals come inside...'

'Oh, dear,' said Paula. 'Do you want to put a canvas over your car, Rafe? We have some spare covers in the garage that we bought after last year's big blow. I know it's only a rental, but heaven knows what this dust might do if it gets into the engine.'

Jennifer stopped what she was doing, aghast at the tacit invitation contained in the suggestion, but before she could think of an objection Rafe turned from the darkening view and strolled back to smile down at his eager hostess.

'I suppose that would be a good idea, but I don't want to impose, Paula.' His diffidence was a beautifully calculated pre-emptive strike. 'I know you weren't expecting me, and Susie told me when I arrived that you had a full complement of guests. Actually, since I wasn't quite sure of the set-up here, or what Jennifer's immediate plans were, I *had* made a reservation at a hotel...'

'Rafe! Of *course* you'll stay here with us!' Paula was visibly shocked by his offer. 'We always have room for *family*, no matter how full we are. Jenny has a lovely big bedroom which takes up the whole of the upstairs, with *en suite* bathroom and outside access via the balcony, so you can both have tons of privacy. Goodness!' she laughed, as the loaded tea tray crashed back down onto the coffee table. 'Jenny would never forgive me if I tried to chase you away—look at her face, she's horrified at the very thought!'

Rafe knew full well what she was horrified by, and it wasn't the thought of their separation.

'But, Mum…' Jennifer was fast running out of spontaneous inventions. A contagious disease? A fear of heights? What reason could she dredge up for her pretend husband not sharing her room? She wracked her brain for inspiration. How about a pathological fear of being murdered in her bed?

Bed? A wave of heat flowed over her body. Oh, God, her mother expected her not just to share a room but to *sleep* with him, in the euphemistic as well as the literal sense. Her breath began to labour in and out of her lungs, as if she was outside, inhaling the smothering ash. She looked at the tall man in his stylishly casual clothes, the easy stance and confident set of his shoulders, the careless good looks, and simmered with hot resentment.

He had apparently earned a small fortune as a model when he was in his late teens and early twenties, enough to subsequently set himself up in the publishing business without using a penny of his father's money or a shred of his influence, and it was obvious why he had been so favoured for spreads in *GQ* and *Vogue*. He oozed a kind of universal sex appeal, attractive to both men and women. And that was with his clothes on!

Jennifer's knees weakened at the impossible task her mother had unknowingly set her. She was supposed to go to bed with *that* and *not* think of sex?

'Now, Jen, I know what you're going to say, but Dot and I can handle the guests.' Her mother interrupted her scurrying thoughts with unaccustomed decisiveness. 'You don't seem to like to admit it, but we managed perfectly well for ourselves during those two months that you were in England. You just devote yourself to getting to know your husband again. After all, considering how little time you've spent together as a married couple, you're still practically honeymooners…'

'Why, so we are,' purred Rafe, moving over to Jennifer and sliding his long arm around her waist, hugging her to his side while he nuzzled the side of her head, lowering his voice to a murmur.

'Just think of it, darling—the two of us up there all alone in your lovely, cosy eyrie, exploring each other's wants and needs...' His warm breath hummed in her ear, lapping at her senses and teasing her overheated imagination. 'Rather like the fantasies I used to weave for myself during those long, languid, steamy Amazon nights...when I'd lie awake, staring into the velvet-black darkness, aching with loneliness, yearning for the touch of a passionate woman...*my* woman...'

He nipped suddenly at her ear and laughed softly as she gave a little squeak, furious with herself for being momentarily seduced by his evocative words into forgetting who and what he was. She, of all people, should know better than to get carried away by his technical mastery of a few seductive phrases. Taken individually, they weren't even particularly *clever* ones...

Jennifer wriggled out of his grasp and found her mother and Dot exchanging silently satisfied looks. She hoped they hadn't caught the substance of Rafe's words, although they had undoubtedly understood the context.

'I'd better clean these up so the kitchen's clear for you to think about dinner, Mum,' she muttered, bending for the tray.

'Here, let me help you with that; you don't seem to be having much luck with crockery today.' Rafe hefted the tray and swivelled it on one flat palm, high above Jennifer's safe reach. 'I was a waiter, too, during my misspent youth,' he told the two older women with a grin. 'Anything to thwart my father's attempts to send me to med school. So, if you need a silver service while I'm here, I'd be delighted to go through my paces.'

Out in the kitchen, Jennifer wrenched on the hot tap and bundled the cups from the tray into the sink with some liquid detergent. 'Did you *have* to play up to them like that?' she sizzled, under cover of the running water.

'Would you rather I bit and snarled and knocked you around so they'd pity you for the brute you married?'

'Yes!'

'Liar. That would horribly upset your mother and that's the last thing you want. This whole charade is to stop her worrying about you. She has absolutely no idea what you're really like, has she?'

Jennifer ignored the comment. It was far too apt, in more ways than he would ever know. She concentrated angrily on the dishes, damning him for being so perceptive. For good or bad they were now co-conspirators, and she would be cutting her own throat if she was *too* antagonistic.

'How did you find me?' She and Sebastian had deliberately avoided mentioning exactly where they had met, and when asked where she was from Jennifer had merely said she was born in Auckland. She had wanted a permanent barrier between her New Zealand and English lives.

'My father's credit card receipts. I found one from Beech House amongst his things a few weeks ago, and recognised your signature from the register office,' he said, revealing he had not only sharp eyes but an excellent visual memory. 'Why did you tell Paula it was *me* you'd married?'

'Believe me, I wish I hadn't,' she said fervently as she rapped a foamy cup upside down onto the tiled bench.

'Careful, you'll chip them if you throw them around like that,' said Rafe, whipping a teatowel off the wall-hook beside the oven and beginning to dry with the comfortable ease of a man used to doing his own domestic chores.

There was a strained silence for a few moments, and

just as it began to get on Jennifer's overstretched nerves he chuckled.

'The Amazon? Couldn't you think of anywhere more remote and inaccessible to send me?' His amused sarcasm drifted into teasing provocation. 'I suppose your ultimate aim was to have me eaten by piranhas during my morning swim in the river.'

'Actually, we were just going to slowly drift out of love under the pressure of the long separation,' she gritted. 'But I must admit that the thought of having you swallowed alive by a giant anaconda had a certain tempting appeal!'

This time his laugh was full-throated. 'Well, you'd better tell me what I was supposed to be doing on this famous expedition, just in case anyone starts asking me for details.'

'You won't be here long enough for them to ask,' she argued.

'Well, I'm certainly not going anywhere while this lasts.' He nodded out of the window at the gritty fog which was continuing to darken the afternoon. His parked car was already coated with a thickly stippled layer of grey-brown volcanic dust. 'I know you'd prefer me permanently out of the way, but even you can't expect me to ignore traffic warnings and risk *real* death for the sake of your personal convenience.'

Reluctantly Jennifer described the fictitious trip she had created, and the function that her 'husband' was supposed to fulfil.

'Photographer! I don't know a thing about cameras!'

'You modelled—you ran a magazine—'

'Neither of which actually involved me getting behind the camera and taking the shots!'

She was irritated by his condescending amusement. 'Well, I know you run several companies now, but I don't think Sebastian ever said what it is you actually *do* every day.' Only that it was very profitable. And Jennifer had resolutely avoided showing any curiosity in that direction. 'So I just drew on your background—I said freelance photography was a sideline of yours.'

'I see. I'm the artistic type. Currently respectable...but with plenty of potential to turn out to be a selfish, self-absorbed swine, constantly pursuing my own goals at the expense of yours,' he guessed shrewdly. 'What else did you make up about me that I should be warned about?'

'Nothing,' she said sullenly. 'I knew the less I said the better.'

She finished the last teaspoon and pulled the plug out of the sink.

'Do Paula and Dot know you're pregnant?'

She angled her stubborn chin at him. 'Of course they do.'

With a genuine wedding ring on her finger, Jennifer had had no hesitation in telling her mother the good news, and, as she had anticipated, Paula had been frankly delighted for her, knowing that her daughter's romantic daydreams had always included a family of her own.

'No "of course" about it, where you're involved,' said Rafe drily. 'Do they think *I* still don't know? Is that why neither of them congratulated me on my impending fatherhood?'

She nodded briefly. In abstract she had accepted that this man was the progenitor of her child, but the concrete reality was still something she avoided. 'I said I didn't find out until after you'd left.'

'So at least you didn't make me the kind of cad who'd run out on his *pregnant* new wife to pursue his own dreams.' He tossed the damp towel onto the bench and leaned one hip against the tiles, his mocking gaze darkening as it ran over her body, lingering on her breasts and reminding her of his earlier outrageousness.

'Well...go ahead, do your duty. Tell your husband he's going to be a daddy...'

A heavy tread made them both turn towards the door. It was Dot, carrying two disposable protective masks.

'I'm just going out to check my plants and call the cats. Do you want to come and get that car-cover with me first, Rafe? Then Jenny can show you around and you can settle in.'

'Sure.' He straightened, taking one of the masks. 'Would you like me to help you look for the animals?'

Dot took a can of fishy catfood from the fridge. 'They'll come pretty quick if I give them a whiff of this; it's so potent we should always wear a mask when we dish it out!'

'See you soon, darling.' Taking Jennifer by surprise, Rafe chucked her under the chin and brushed a light kiss across her startled mouth as he exited, leaving her glaring after him, scrubbing furiously at the tingling brand. The fleeting kiss he had given her at her wedding, when that embarrassing photo had been taken, had been equally disturbing, and after that she had been even more careful to avoid his company. Now there would be no avoiding him, and by her own words she had condemned herself to allowing him to touch her whenever he liked...at least in public.

His suspicion, his bitterness, his contempt she could fight with reciprocal fierceness, but her defences were proving alarmingly vulnerable to his mocking humour, his quick intelligence and his sheer physical attractiveness.

Frowning, she quickly put the dried crockery away and went back to the living room, to find her mother unwinding the draught excluders that would stop the windblown ash from seeping in through the doors and windows.

'I see Rafe's bags are still out in the hall. Do you

want to tidy your room before you take him up?' Paula asked, adding teasingly, 'Just in case there's anything lying around you don't want him to see. I know there are always *some* cosmetic secrets a woman likes to keep beyond the first few weeks of her marriage—'

The words were hardly out of her mouth before Jennifer dashed out of the room and up the stairs, her heart pounding. How could she have forgotten?

The sloping ceilings of the converted attic framed the friendly clutter of the room. Two dormer windows and bi-folding glass doors opening out onto a wooden balcony facing the mountain let in plenty of light to counteract the effect of dark wooden plank walls and ceiling. A squat double bed, an old-fashioned mirrored wardrobe and matching dressing table, a big bookcase and a large battered desk and chair were the main pieces of furniture.

Jennifer ran over to the desk on which her budget computer had pride of place. She knew she couldn't rely on Rafe not to snoop and pry into every corner of her existence if he felt like it, so she quickly sat down and turned on the computer, mentally calculating how long it would take him to tie down a loose tarpaulin over his car as she deleted large chunks of her hard-copy files, safe in the knowledge that they were already doubly backed up onto floppies.

While the computer was chomping its way down the list she emptied all red-labelled floppy disks from the plastic box beside the screen and bundled them into her underwear drawer, wrapping them securely in an unattractive woollen spencer before pushing them deep to the back of her bras and undies. Then she gathered cardboard hanging files out of the bottom drawer of her desk and stuffed them, papers, files and all, into the slit between the wall and the back of the heavy oak wardrobe. Heaven knew how she was going to get them out again!

Fortunately she had formed the cautious habit of always cleaning up very thoroughly after herself every time she worked at the computer, and personally burning the contents of her wastepaper bin in the outside incinerator, so it wasn't long before all that remained on her computer and desk was information regarding the running of Beech House that would probably bore Rafe to tears.

She stood for a moment in the centre of the room, nervously shifting from foot to foot, double-checking that there was nothing else she had forgotten, her roving eyes deliberately avoiding the big, soft feather bed.

The books! Even if Rafe wasn't much of a reader himself he was clever enough to know that he could learn something about her character from the type of books she kept.

She swept a section from the middle row off the shelf, and one or two others at random, and dumped them into her wicker laundry basket, heaping her soiled clothes over the top. With luck Rafe would be gone before the next wash. If not—*no*, she refused to even contemplate not being able to persuade him to leave.

There!

Not a sign that the bedroom was inhabited by anything other than a normal, ordinary, twenty-seven-year-old woman of average, everyday tastes who had nothing to hide.

She just hoped that Raphael Jordan could be persuaded to believe the evidence of his own eyes!

CHAPTER FOUR

JENNIFER tried to look relaxed as Raphael dropped his soft-sided suitcase and expensive leather roll-bag under the dormer window and circled around her bedroom, his head tilted and eyes half-closed, almost as if he was tasting the air. He made her aware of the soft mingling of subtle feminine scents—lavender from the perfumed paper with which she lined her clothes drawers, a woodsy sweetness from the dish of dried petals on the bookshelf, rose from the lingering fragrance of her morning shower and hints of a darker, more sensuous floral tone from a spilled perfume bottle on the dressing table.

He ran his finger moodily along the outer edge of her pristine desk, lifted frosted make-up bottles on the dressing table, opened her wardrobe to inspect the contents and stepped into the adjoining bathroom, with its polished rimu cabinetry and deep, claw-footed white bath, with a modern, hand-held brass shower spray hooked high on the wall above the vintage brass taps.

On the way back out he passed the laundry basket, and in her nervous state of heightened anxiety Jennifer half expected him to lift the lid and rummage inside to find the evidence of her secret notoriety.

As she had expected, he stopped before the bookcase for the longest time, absently toying with the dish of petals as he studied the titles, an eclectic array of fiction and non-fiction, classic and contemporary, treasure and trash.

'You like to read,' he pronounced with faintly surprised satisfaction, stroking the flowing gilt inscription on the spine of a vintage cloth Bible. 'Have you read this?'

She was wary of the innocuousness of his question. Nothing about Raphael Jordan was harmless. 'Most of it. My father was a minister—'

'Was?'

'He drowned when I was nineteen, saving the life of a young boy who was swept off rocks at a surf beach.' Her quiet pride in her father's impulsive act of self-sacrifice was evident in the soft lilt of her voice. 'He worked amongst the local parishes here. We grew up helping him search out his readings and themes for his sermons.'

Rafe turned. 'We?'

'My brother, Ian, and I. He was a year younger than me. He was killed in a car accident seven years ago. That was when my mother damaged her back…'

She looked away from the penetrating green stare, remembering the tragedy of that day and the added anguish six months later when her fiancé, who had been the driver of the car in which they had all been travelling, had been unable to handle his guilt and had broken off their engagement.

Rafe saw the tightening crook of her wide mouth, and the distant, unfocused look in her brown eyes as they suddenly evaded his, and wondered with a renewed burst of savage frustration what else she was holding back. He wanted to stride over and seize her by her soft shoulders and shake her until she rattled, spilling out all her secrets, but he had already decided that guile was more effective than force where she was concerned.

The more he found out about this infuriating woman the less he felt he knew her. His angry preconceptions had begun to crumble from the moment that he had held her, soft, limp and helpless in his arms. Unconscious,

she had been totally vulnerable, unable to protect herself
or the baby nestling inside her ripening body.

His baby.

Ignorance no longer protected him from the consequences of his impulsive act of reckless defiance.
However artificial the method of conception, thanks to
his father's unethical revelation there was no retreating
from the knowledge that part of Raphael was now part
of Jennifer, and vice versa.

So, who was she?

Was she a cunning, money-grubbing, conscienceless
bitch? Or a foolishly misguided innocent? A hard-
hearted, clear-thinking opportunist? Or an impulsive
woman who had confused wealth with security and pan-
icked when her rash decision landed her in over her
head? Or perhaps she was a combination of all of those
things.

It would have suited him to have her as black as she
had been painted by his rampaging ex-stepmothers and
their ravening hordes. By the time he had finally tracked
Jennifer down he had been in a killing black fury, the
blade of his rage honed and sharpened by three months
of torrid internecine warfare amongst the various competing Jordan factions trying to overturn Sebastian's
will.

There had been threats of injunctions and court orders,
and unseemly scuffles in the lawyers' offices, until it was
made clear that the old man had sewed everything up
watertight, even to the point of having an independent
psychiatric report done which attested to his mental
health at the time he had amended his will. Any legal
challenge to his final wishes and most of the estate
would go to charity. So the scavengers had finally settled
for their assigned portions—which had been fair, even
generous, if not as lavish as they would have liked.

As the only blood heir, Rafe was unable to avoid being tainted by the ugliness, and even though he knew that the same scenario would have been played out by his rapacious relatives *whatever* had been in Sebastian's will, he had focused his anger on Jennifer. She had become the repository for his deeply conflicted feelings about his father. When he had set out from London he had been headed towards a confrontation with the past, and now that he had run slap-bang into the future he was still groping to reconcile the two.

He watched Jennifer nervously brush at the fringe that feathered her pale forehead as she realised he was still staring at her. She got very uneasy if he looked at her for any sustained length of time. When he had first met her in London he had thought it was shyness, but when he had seen her coolly out-staring some of his obnoxious stepbrothers he had realised that her uneasiness was a much less innocent form of awareness.

He pulled his wandering thoughts back into line, calculating the facts. Her father had died when she was nineteen, and a year later she had lost her only brother...and been left with a disabled mother. That gave him an inkling as to the reason Jennifer had never finished her nursing training. He already knew how protective she was towards her mother.

'And she's been in a wheelchair ever since? Is she completely paralysed from the waist down?'

Jennifer looked at him in surprise. 'Oh, no—Mum can walk...some of the time she doesn't even have to use her stick. But she still has bad bouts of chronic pain and weakness in her legs, and at those times it's easier to use the wheelchair. It gives her back a rest and it's safer than her staggering about, risking a fall. Sometimes it happens when she's overdone things, or is tired, and at other times for no reason that she can explain.' A shadow passed over her expression. 'She's had several operations over the years, but there was so little improvement after the last two that the doctors say it's no use trying any more corrective surgery. At least there's no sign of progressive degeneration of the spine, so it shouldn't get any worse than it is now. Not that that's much consolation for Mum...'

'She seems a very happy, well-adjusted person.'

She thought he was still talking about her mother's injuries. 'She is.'

'So why bother with all the complicated lying?' he continued in the same even tone. 'Why not simply tell her that you were marrying Sebastian?'

'Because she would have known it wasn't for love!' Paula would have been deeply shocked by the idea of her daughter marrying Sebastian, and even more appalled if she'd discovered the reasons behind it.

'Then why mention getting married at all?'

'I was going to have a baby, that's why! I couldn't arrive home pregnant *and* unmarried after only a couple of months away,' she said, exasperated by his blank look. Of course, in the trendy circles in which he *had* moved, unmarried mothers were probably the norm. 'I couldn't do that to Mum. This is small-town New Zealand. People gossip and they have long memories. She and Dad always set a very moral tone, and Mum is still very active in the local church...'

'Well, if you didn't want her to know it was for the money, you could have told her you were doing it out of compassion for a dying man, that it *was* going to be a marriage in name only—which I take it was part of the agreement?'

'And then how would I have explained getting pregnant?' she argued, her question a tacit affirmative to his question.

'What was wrong with the truth? That Sebastian so desperately wanted another child that you entered a programme for infertile couples.'

'Mum doesn't approve of assisted reproductive technology,' she admitted starkly, aware that she could be handing him yet another weapon against her. 'I told you—she has very traditional moral views. She and Sebastian had arguments about it. She thinks it's going against God's will to try and manipulate life. She would have been very hurt and disappointed to think that I...I—'

'That her sweet little girl had decided to go into the lucrative rent-a-womb business?'

After his preceding mildness the harsh interruption was like a dash of acid in Jennifer's face. Before she could summon an equally searing reply he had turned away, as if uninterested in her response, moving over to sit testily on the edge of the bed.

'Well, well...feather mattress?' he asked as he sank down into the deep softness that lay atop the slatted wooden frame. His laced suede walking boots planted firmly on the floor, he let himself fall back, spread-eagled, onto the smooth, cream duvet, staring up at the rimu ceiling.

'The last time I lay on one of these was in Switzerland, at a tiny little country inn. Best night's sleep I ever had in my life,' he gloated.

The bed had puffed up around him, almost swallowing him from sight, so Jennifer's view of him was reduced to a pair of spread thighs angling to a V at the centre of his body, where the denim ridged over a firm bulge. It was a disturbingly erotic image of anonymous male sexuality.

Did he *have* to flaunt himself like that? she thought furiously. Did he think she didn't already have *enough* proof of his fabulous virility?

'Well, don't get too excited about it because *you're* sleeping on the floor,' she informed him.

He pushed up onto his hands, catching the direction

of her offended glare. His green eyes mocked her flustered expression as he casually hooked one foot behind his other knee, widening his thighs in an even more blatant display of his undisputed manhood.

'Maybe I won't feel like sleeping at all tonight,' he murmured with an insinuating smile.

She stiffened. She knew she shouldn't but she had to ask. 'What do you mean?' she burst out aggressively.

His spiky blond hair provided a ruffled halo to his exaggerated expression of innocence. 'Only that if the mountain blows its top I'd like to see it happen. We'll be able to keep watch all night from up here, won't we? From where I am now, the summit is in a perfect frame.' He nodded towards the glass doors parallel to the bed. Having positioned the bed in precisely that place so that she could lie there in the mornings, dreamily contemplating the sheer majesty of nature, Jennifer didn't even have to look to check that he was right.

Rafe had already turned his attention to something else. He was sliding open the drawer of her small bedside table and peering interestedly at the jumbled contents. She hurried over but she was too late. One eyebrow quirked and he lifted out a wood-framed photograph, shaking off a sprinkle of elastic hairbands and clips that had littered its surface.

'So this is where you keep me. I'm sure your mother implied I was prominently on display...'

'She hardly ever comes up here—the stairs are too difficult for her,' snapped Jennifer. 'Anyway, *she* respects my privacy too much to pry.'

'So I was relegated to out of sight, out of mind, hmm?'

If only it had been so easy! Jennifer watched in frustration as he dusted the glass with the edge of his sleeve and propped the photo on the table, between the small shaded lamp and the cream telephone.

'I don't remember seeing you wear spectacles when you were in England,' he mused, glancing from the photograph to her annoyed face.

'I usually wear contact lenses, but with all the volcanic dust in the air right now...' She shrugged, her average looks never having given her much cause for vanity.

'They make you appear quite bookish...but then you are, aren't you? I can't figure you out. Your wardrobe here is full of home-made clothes, but in London you wore smart labels—abandoned along with your husband. Over there you were always demure and polite, no matter what the provocation; here you lash out. In London you only admitted to being an unqualified nurse; in New Zealand you're an experienced inn-keeper. Which is the *real* Jennifer, I wonder?'

'Everyone has different facets to their personality that are revealed in different situations,' she said stiffly, thinking that even *she* wasn't sure who the real Jennifer was any more.

'So they do. I look forward to exploring more of your...revealing facets.' Her watched her mouth prim, her eyes flash, and flicked a finger at her blushing cheek in the photograph.

'Amazing how deceptive appearances can be, isn't it?' he said drily. 'How it must have bruised Sebastian's ego to see himself edited out of his own wedding picture...or didn't he know about this little game of musical husbands you played for your mother?'

'Of course he did; it was his i—' She stopped and Rafe's eyes narrowed.

'Idea,' he finished slowly, when she showed no signs of going on. 'My *father* suggested you use me as a substitute?' By the end of the sentence his incredulity had risen to sharp suspicion.

Alarmed, she tried to step back, but he caught her

narrow wrist, bending it back until she was forced to sink to her knees in front of him to relieve the uncomfortable pressure on her arm.

'He— He thought that it would be easier to borrow an identity than to invent a completely new one and then have to make up a whole lot more lies to remember,' she stammered, as he eased the pressure just enough to act as a leash. 'He said that if I used you I wouldn't have to lie about my new surname. A-and he said that it would reassure Mum to know that I hadn't been swept off my feet by a complete stranger, but someone whose background she was aware of...'

It had seemed such a good idea at the time, and one that Sebastian had claimed had very little risk of discovery. Part of their infamous bargain had included Jennifer's mother being kept strictly in the dark. They had both known that Paula would have been deeply worried by her daughter's marriage to Sebastian, and equally appalled if she had ever learned the reasons behind it.

'Since I'd always planned to come straight back here after Sebastian died, there was no reason why you and Mum should ever have had any contact,' she finished weakly.

'And then a fictitious divorce from your fictitious husband and everybody's happy!' he grunted. 'I take it your mother has more liberal views on divorce than she does on marriage and procreation?'

'Well, even the church recognises irretrievable breakdown,' she muttered. Her mother would have been disappointed but, with a long, gentle tapering off, hardly devastated.

'And what about the baby? The unfortunate bargaining chip in all of this? What was it agreed you would do with *my* baby after Sebastian died?'

'Nothing... I mean, he knew I was going to bring it

up here, of course,' she said huskily. 'He knew that I'd be a good mother—'

'And a *father* didn't matter? What if something happened to *you*, for God's sake!' he exploded, jerking her wrist and leaning forward to thrust his face fiercely close to hers. 'Don't you think Paula would have wanted to contact me *then*? Even if I'd never demonstrated a shred of interest in the child before, your mother still might have considered that I had the right to know. Or wouldn't it have mattered what a bloody mess you left behind you, as long as you had everything you wanted while you were alive?'

Jennifer blanched. She had never even considered the possibility. Under the rules of donor IVF programmes the biological parents had no legal access or responsibility, and, anyway, in her own mind the baby had always been hers and hers alone. Both the nominal and the biological father had been irrelevant. If anything happened to her she vaguely assumed that her mother would have sole legal guardianship—but of course Paula thought that it had been an entirely natural conception...

'Oh, God,' she breathed, her free hand moving to her stomach. She couldn't believe how short-sighted she had been—no, how utterly blind in her pursuit of her goal.

The movement dragged Rafe's eyes away from her face, and he suddenly cursed virulently under his breath and dropped her wrist as if it was hot coal. She sat back on her heels, rubbing at the faint red weals on her tender skin. He got up and paced, running a hand down the back of his neck, and Jennifer got shakily to her feet, uncertain of her next move.

'What a mess! What a crazy bloody mess!' Rafe ground out. 'I still don't understand it! If everything was going as planned, why did you have to run away like a thief in the night? That certainly put a kink in your image as a caring wife. What were you afraid might happen after he died? Everything was legal. You had the money. And you had no way of knowing that he'd told me the baby was mine, because I was the last one to see him alive.'

She jumped as he prowled back to stand in front of her, hands on his hips, streaks of temper across his hard cheekbones.

'Tell me this one thing straight at least: if Sebastian hadn't suffered his deathbed crisis of conscience, would *you* ever have told me that my "half-brother" or "half-sister" was in fact my own child?'

'I— I don't know—'

'You don't know.' It was repeated with such contempt that she knew he didn't believe her. 'Come on, you must have *thought* about it. Maybe you figured that if you ever milked the trust dry you could turn up and black-mail *me* for child support.'

'No! I never thought— Maybe if— Oh!' She raised her hands and covered her distraught face. She didn't know how much it was safe to admit. How much to trust him.

'Oh, I don't know *what* I was going to do! How could I know? How could I possibly have known that—' She put her clenched fist to her mouth, biting down on the words, her brown eyes dark with anguished doubt.

'How could you have known—what? Jennifer?' He pulled the gag from her mouth, encompassing her entire fist in his warm hand. *'How could you have known what?'*

But the moment of revelation had passed. Jennifer had herself under control again, albeit very shaky control.

'That it was all going to come apart at the seams like this,' she whispered.

The dark gold stubble on his lower cheeks glinted as his jaw muscles clenched. He lifted her fist and pressed his mouth to the tiny indentations created by her teeth, his lips brushing in a mocking salute across the gold wedding band on her third finger before letting her go.

'Lies usually do, especially the kind of whoppers you've been telling.'

'Oh, right, and I suppose you've never told a lie in your life,' she said sarcastically, wiping her fingers on her trousers to try and rid herself of his lingering touch. 'You were doing pretty well there downstairs, for an amateur...'

'I'm reasonably proficient with a social lie, but, no, until I met you I'd actually considered myself to be quite painfully honest—especially in my relationships with women.'

He bent to his suitcase, unzipping the top and flinging it back, pawing through the neatly packed clothes. He threw a pair of black jeans and a thin black knitted jumper over the back of her desk chair and pulled his cream sweater over his head, dumping it back on top of the unzipped suitcase. Underneath he was wearing a white silk shirt with pearlised buttons, which he began to flick open with one hand. As the shirt parted she could see that the hair on his chest was one shade darker than that on his head. It grew in flattened swirls around his dark, masculine nipples and created a thick mat over his rippling pectorals. His evenly tanned skin was sleek and glossy, glowing with health.

'What are you doing?' she asked, her eyes darting nervously past him to the bed.

He dealt with his cuffs and divested himself of the shirt before he spoke, now bare to the low-slung belt of his snug jeans.

'I've been travelling non-stop for over twenty-four hours. I'm grimy, I'm tired and I'm angry—and I can do something about at least two of the three. I'm going to strip, shower, nap and change into fresh clothes—in that order. If you want to stand there and watch, feel free. Or you can join me, if you like…'

His eyes fixed on her, he unclipped his flat gold buckle and stripped his leather belt from its denim loops, folding it to a strop in his hand, which he then struck lightly against his other palm.

He saw Jennifer's eyes widen behind her glasses and growled, 'You needn't look like that; I don't beat my women.'

'I never thought you did,' she defended herself, wondering if he realised what he looked like, standing there stripped to the waist, golden head cocked, his green eyes stoked with insolent challenge, the lean muscles of his arms and torso rippling as he flexed the leather strap. He looked like every woman's fantasy of a dangerous lover. Jennifer's fingers itched for her keyboard, her protection against the pangs of forbidden lust.

'Unless they consider it a stimulating form of fore-play, of course,' Rafe added, with a sultry smoulder designed to get under her creamy skin. 'Then I'm perfectly willing to indulge in a little light bondage and discipline to enhance the lady's pleasure…' He slapped leather to palm again. 'How about you, Jennifer? Do you like your sex strictly straight—or with an intriguing twist?'

She was shattered by the question and it showed. Shattered but not shocked, Rafe's keenly developed sexual instincts told him, and he felt a hot throb of curiosity thicken his loins. Then his anger kicked in, snarling through his veins. Dammit, he *wanted* her to be shocked. He wanted her to feel tormented, as the thought of *her* had tormented *him* for the last few months. He wanted her to be eminently shockable, so that he could have the satisfaction of making her pay in some small measure for all the trouble that she had caused him, and *would* cause him…

'Maybe you just like to watch, hmm?' He dropped his

belt and boldly unzipped his jeans. 'Is this what you're waiting for, Mrs Jordan?' he jeered, sliding his hands inside the denim to cup himself.

That got her!

She gasped, blushing furiously, and backed away, almost stumbling over Rafe's roll-bag and losing a flat shoe. He withdrew his hands and bent to toss his bag out of the way while she frantically nudged her loose shoe back onto her foot and continued to skitter towards the door.

'Not going to join me in the shower, then?' he said, sauntering after her fleeing figure, his unsnapped jeans peeled back to reveal silky white briefs which brazenly outlined the contours of his semi-arousal.

'I'm told I give *incredibly* good showers...'

Jennifer was *incredibly* proud of herself for keeping her eyes firmly at chest level.

'In that case I'm sure you'll remember to wash your mouth out with soap while you're in there!' she said, as her hip bumped the door handle and she grabbed at it, spinning to safety and slamming the door behind her.

She might have had the last word but it didn't feel like it as his mocking laughter, muffled by the solid door, followed her down the stairs. He had routed her from her own private territory and he knew it!

It took a good hour of solid dusting and stuffing of draught excluders into every structural chink and crack that she could find for her to cool off. It didn't help that while she was doing the kitchen her mother, chopping vegetables for dinner on a specially lowered section of bench, wanted to rhapsodise about how nice he was, how intelligent and articulate, interesting and amusing, and terribly, terribly sexy...

'Mum!'

'Well, so he is, darling. I'd have to be blind not to notice.' Paula heaved a sigh. In her softly draped blue dress, with spiral tendrils of her long brown hair escaping from the plump chignon at the back of her head, she looked exactly what she was—a hopeless romantic.

'And that secret smoulder in his eyes whenever he looks at you—as if he's longing to pounce on you and eat you up!'

Jennifer shivered. Chew her up and spit her out, more like!

Dot brought in the cats—Maxie, the lazy white Persian, looking extremely disgruntled at the disruption to his afternoon snooze as he was carried off to the laundry for an extra grooming of his long, grit-laden fur, and Milo, the short-haired Burmese-cross, sneezing when the panting golden Labrador which had bounced in at Dot's heels thumped down on the floor and began scratching vigorously, raising a cloud of dust around the disdainful chocolate nose.

'Bonzer!' Jennifer tugged him to his feet by his brown leather collar. 'Go into the laundry with Dot and she'll give you a brush. *Then* you can scratch.'

Since they were fed in there, 'laundry' was a word both animals associated with food, and they responded with amusing alacrity, as usual Milo getting there first by taking a shortcut under Paula's chair while Bonzer, whose enthusiasm outran his intelligence, took the corner too fast and surfed the mat into the wall before rebounding out of sight with a sheepish bark.

Jennifer got out the vacuum cleaner to whisk across the kitchen floor, and then figured she might as well do the rest of the ground floor. Anything to take her mind off the man upstairs.

The temperature continued to drop rapidly as the afternoon moved into evening and the mountain continued to push more dense clouds of black ash high into the atmosphere, blotting out the remaining warmth of the sun. Wearing a mask that couldn't obscure the sour smell of sulphur in the air, Jennifer went out to the woodshed behind the garage and brought in several loads of split and round logs and a scuttle of coal. She restoked the small pot-belly stove in the dining room and lit the fire she had reset that morning in the grate of the huge stone fireplace in the living room.

Dot took her camera out onto the verandah and took several shots of the new cloud formations, part of her project to document the progress of the eruption in her daily journal. Then she helped Jennifer disconnect the pipes from the roof to the concrete water-tank, to make sure that their water supply didn't get contaminated if it rained and the compacted ash in the gutters washed into the system. Fortunately the tank was fairly full, and Jennifer was confident that with careful usage they wouldn't run out before the crisis passed.

The phone shrilled several times as the local grapevine swung into action and friends and acquaintants passed on information and gossip about the latest developments, and Jennifer was unsurprised when the Carters phoned to say they'd heard the warnings on the radio and decided to remain in Taupo for the night and drive back the next day, conditions permitting.

Jennifer's brief flare of elation died as she realised that there was no way to suggest Rafe use the unexpected extra bed without raising awkward questions about her marriage. And she couldn't see him meekly agreeing to sneak down under cover of darkness—or allowing her to do it. He had no intention of making things easier for her.

She went to tell her mother about the Carters and found herself quizzed about Rafe's food preferences as Paula pondered over the next day's menu.

'What about chicken? He must like chicken,' Paula said as the list of 'don't knows' grew. She leafed through the recipe book she had open on the dining room table.

'*I* never saw him eat it,' Jennifer said truthfully. She had dined with him a few times in Sebastian's company, but had always been too self-conscious, too tensely aware of his cynical gaze, to pay any attention to what they were eating. The atmosphere between father and son had been none too conducive to digestion, either. Their relationship seemed to be based more on tolerance than affection, and although there was a certain mutual respect it was strictly man-to-man rather than father-to-son. They held opposing views on almost everything, and Sebastian's habit of hammering endlessly at his point in order to prod a reaction out of Rafe only served to make his son withdraw deeper into the cynical indifference that infuriated the father.

'I think he likes sweetbreads, brains, liver, ox-heart—things like that,' she said, in a burst of malicious inspiration.

Paula's brow wrinkled. 'Offal, you mean?'

Jennifer grinned. 'Yes.'

Her mother tapped her pencil against her greying temple, looking dubious. 'Are you sure, dear? He just doesn't look the offal type.'

'What type do *you* think he is?'

'Oh…hot and spicy, sharp and crunchy—he looks as if he'd enjoy Thai food and pickles.'

The comparison made Jennifer's tastebuds tingle. He had certainly been hot and spicy earlier. 'What a weird combination!' she joked, to hide her chagrin.

'Speaking of which, have you told him about the baby yet?'

When Jennifer hesitated, Paula sped happily on to her own answer. 'No, of course not—you wouldn't want to hit him over the head with the news while he was still groggy from jet lag. You want to savour it…set the mood. Maybe tonight, when you go upstairs together…'

Later, as early dusk set in and Jennifer was setting the table, Paula fretted.

'Don't you think you've let him sleep long enough? I know he's travelled a long way but they say the best way to combat jet lag is to try to keep as closely as possible to your new destination's time frame. Anyway, that leg of lamb will be ready soon, and I'm sure he'll be hungry after all that plastic airline food. Why don't you go and wake him up?'

Because Jennifer infinitely preferred him solidly unconscious. She wasn't looking forward to the four of them sitting down to a cosy family dinner. And she *especially* didn't want to go upstairs and see him lying like an arrogant lord in *her* bed. Probably nude. Oh, yes, he would love it if she went upstairs to wake him up—it would give him another chance to embarrass and humiliate her by flaunting his brazen sexuality.

'Um, he said to let him sleep until he wakes,' she said, adding another lie to the long list that had already imperilled her soul.

'If he wakes up *too* rested he won't want to sleep tonight,' her mother pointed out, then realised what she'd said. Her eyes crinkled. 'Oh! Is *that* why you're letting him sleep!'

'He said he'd like to watch if the volcano goes up,' said Jennifer severely.

'Well, of course, dear, that's what I meant,' said Paula blandly, handing her the table napkins from the sideboard. 'He's very well travelled, isn't he, your Rafe—all those other volcanic regions he's been…I know you said that after he got the Amazon thing out of his system he wanted to settle down here in New Zealand, but sometimes once that sort of adventuring gets into the blood…well, just look at Dot—sixty-five and still backpacking her way to far-flung places!'

Another lie coming home to roost. But Jennifer saw a chance to turn it to her advantage.

'Rafe knows that this is where I want to bring up my child.' That much at least was true. 'He knows that you and I run this place as a team, and that I would never leave you in the lurch...' She owed her mother the reassurance that she would not be left alone in the twilight of her life. If not for Jennifer's former fiancé, Paula would probably have had a daughter-in-law and other grandchildren by now.

'The best time to travel with children is when they're little, and you don't have to worry about regular schooling,' Paula said wistfully. 'I would have liked to have been able to do that. I sometimes think it would have been nice if your father had been a missionary, rather than a parish minister. Not that I regretted marrying him for a moment—there's no substitute for love.'

Jennifer only vaguely registered what her mother was saying as she timidly began to lay the groundwork for future disillusionment.

'I sometimes wonder if—Rafe being so...so sophisticated and so much more *exciting* than me—if—well, he might end up finding me boring. I mean, when I look at us together I wonder what a fantastic guy like him sees in someone as ordinary as me...'

Paula clicked her tongue reprovingly. 'Jenny! You're not ordinary—you're unique—the only you in the entire universe. You're a warm, loving, loyal, compassionate and caring young woman, and *any* man would consider himself fortunate to have you in his life!'

'Believe me, I do.'

Jenny's heart leapt into her throat as she saw Rafe standing in the doorway, clad in the black clothes he had draped across the chair, the long sleeves of the V-necked sweater pushed up his strong forearms to bunch at his elbows.

'I can't tell you how *fortunate* I feel to have found Jenny,' he said, moving into the room with an easy stride. He looked well rested, alert and dangerously determined as he rounded the table and homed in on his target. He reached for Jennifer, sliding firm hands around her narrow waist and pulling her towards him until their thighs clashed, bending his head so that his mouth slowly approached hers.

'And before tonight is over I'll make very sure that she knows exactly where she belongs in my life!'

CHAPTER FIVE

RAFE'S lips were only a breath away when a burst of activity in the hall rescued Jennifer from her mesmerised state. She quickly turned her head aside so that his mouth landed on her ear.

He nuzzled it softly, his fingers tightening on her waist as she stiffened.

While her mother manoeuvred her chair to investigate the raised voices, Rafe took shameless advantage of the chance to tease his 'wife'.

'Sophisticated, exciting, fantastic...?' he whispered mockingly into the depths of her sensitised ear. 'I had no idea you found me so impressive, darling. You can be sure I'll do my best to live up to my billing!'

Jennifer jerked her head back, glaring at him through stony eyes, fighting her vivid awareness of the iron-hard thighs pushing against her lower body. But before she could utter the words that sizzled on her tongue the cause of the commotion trooped into the room.

It was Dave and Celia Wright, the young couple who were renting the front bedroom. They were freelance documentary-makers making a tourist film about New Zealand ski resorts, and had revelled in the profit to be made from grabbing dramatic news footage.

They were grimy but exhilarated, having come from the east of the mountain where, they reported, the Desert Road, the main arterial route south, had now been closed by the lethal combination of falling ash and black ice forming on the snow-banked road. They had stopped in for a quick shower and change, and to pick up some of their extra gear, before they headed on to tiny

Whakapapa Village, the closest settlement to Ruapehu's northwestern ski slopes, where they had heard rumoured a 'lahar party' was being held in the pub by some of the hundreds of ski workers who had been laid off their seasonal jobs as a result of the closure of the mountain.

When Paula expressed concern about their being on the road at all, let alone at night, Dave shook his shaggy ginger head and pointed out they had the same kind of big four-wheel drive equipped with chains and fog-lights that the rangers and emergency services were using.

'And, besides, we can't afford to let the competition get the jump on us. The place is crawling with press. The TV networks have all got crews roving around out there, but if we get the best pictures, we can beat them out with their own networks, and maybe even CNN.'

Dave's dark blue eyes suddenly focused suspiciously on Rafe, who still had one arm around Jennifer's tense waist, preventing her from easing away.

Rafe grinned, reading his mind. 'It's OK, I'm not a member of the Fourth Estate. Your story lead is safe.'

There was a small, expectant pause, and Jennifer forced a smile. 'Dave and Celia, this is—' How to describe him? She simply couldn't push out the words, and settled for a lame, 'Uh, this is Raphael...'

Rafe had no such qualms. As he shook hands with the couple he paraded the outrageous truth as a silly joke. 'Rafe Jordan—since this delicious hussy claims to be my wife, I guess that leaves me no alternative but to admit that we're related by marriage.'

A faint puff of air punctuated his last word as Jennifer discreetly jabbed a warning elbow into his solar plexus.

'Oh, sorry,' she said, levering herself away with the elbow as he rubbed the tender spot. 'Did I hurt you?'

'Winded rather than wounded, darling,' he said, his tigerish smile carrying a warning of its own. 'And I'm rapidly adjusting to your wicked knack for taking my breath away.'

Celia commented on the heavenly aroma of roast, and, on learning that the Wrights hadn't eaten since they had gulped a hamburger on the run around noon, Paula persuaded the pair to join them for dinner before they rushed off again. It was with relief that Jennifer heard them agree, on the understanding that they would pay extra on the tariff.

At least with Dave and Celia present the conversation wouldn't get too personal, she thought, as the pair went away to clean up and she set two extra places, while Rafe was roped into carving the lamb.

The reality was somewhat different.

Paula explained as they all sat down at the extended oak table, to a succulent roast with all the trimmings, that although Beech House operated as a bed and breakfast, they were willing to negotiate for the provision of other meals, as long as the guests concerned didn't mind eating *en famille*.

'So, if you want a packed lunch, or to eat here in the evening, Celia, you only have to let us know in time to organise it.

'Your father used to have most of his dinners with us, Rafe,' she reminisced, putting Jennifer's nerves immediately onto alert. 'Right from the first time he came here—which was what, Jenny? Just over five years ago now? I suppose she told you the story.' Her thin face softened with her gamine grin as she told the Wrights, 'There was some mix-up at the expensive hotel Sebastian was booked into so he stormed out in a huff and we were the first place he'd phoned that had a vacancy—it was the height of the season.

'I don't think he'd ever stayed at a B&B before, he usually went everywhere first-class, but he really appreciated the personal touch and what he called our "homespun charm''.' She laughed, with a rueful look at Jennifer. 'The surroundings *were* a bit shabby in those pre-renovation days, but he said he liked being made to feel he was part of the family.' She preened faintly. 'He even used to say that it was my fabulous cooking that kept him coming back year after year!'

'Five years?'

Sitting beside Rafe, Jennifer was able to avoid his hard stare, but she couldn't help feeling the tension that entered his body as he sipped from his glass of water—having declined, on the grounds of jet lag, Paula's offer to open a bottle of wine.

As far as anyone in London, including Rafe, had been concerned, she had met Sebastian only weeks before she had married him. He had asked her not to mention their previous, intermittent acquaintance, smugly enjoying the notion of thwarting all attempts to discover any motive in his apparent madness. Since the whole point of his annual month-long overseas holiday had been to get completely away from the stresses and strains of his daily life—including his demanding, dysfunctional extended family—he had always refused to leave a fixed itinerary behind. And Rafe had been unfairly included on his father's information blacklist not, Jennifer suspected, because he had been curious to know where his father went on his trips, but because he so resolutely *hadn't*.

'I don't remember you telling me you'd known him quite *that* long, darling,' Rafe said with studied casualness, and under the table Jennifer felt his long legs shift, his knee brushing up against hers. When she tried to angle her leg away she suddenly felt his hand curling over her wool-clad knee, clamping it to his.

Above the tablecloth he serenely continued to wield his fork, and it became a matter of pride to show that she was unmoved by his threatening touch.

Jennifer shrugged, strands of her silky hair catching against the red angora sweater. Much to her mother's dismay she hadn't changed for dinner—not only because she hadn't wanted to go into her room while Rafe was still there, but because she didn't want him to think she was doing it for *him*…and she would have been, for in the casual tradition of Beech House they rarely dressed for dinner.

'Don't you? I'm sure I must have,' she said off-handedly, taking a sip of her own water, half wishing it was a hefty slug of whisky, except she knew that she needed an exceptionally clear head when dealing with Rafe.

Her punishment was to feel the warm, heavy weight of his hand slide further up her thigh, and she hastily pressed her legs together, unfortunately trapping his fingertips between the tender cushions of her upper thighs. He wiggled his fingers, sending ripples of sensation thrilling up her legs, and when she tried relaxing her muscles just enough to let his fingers slip free he insinuated his touch even higher, so that she quickly had to lock them tight again.

She casually put her hand under the table to fend him off, but even the gouge of her neat, short fingernails into the tender joints of his wrist didn't make him flinch.

Nobody else at the table seemed aware of her impotent squirming, but Jennifer could feel herself beginning to glow like a beacon with anger and embarrassment.

'Gravy, Rafe?' She snatched up the steaming boat and hovered it above the edge of his plate—and his vulnerable lap.

'I already have some, thank you,' he said politely, his green eyes meeting her silent challenge, his hand remaining firmly in possession.

She tilted the gravy boat fractionally but his gaze remained steady, showing not even a flicker of concern that his manhood was in imminent danger of being scalded. What made him so damned certain that she was bluffing?

Maybe the fact that they both knew he held all the cards.

With a sigh she put the gravy boat down and he immediately removed his hand and picked up his knife again, a smile ghosting around the corners of his mouth.

She scowled at him, and he tilted his head in mocking acknowledgement of her unwilling surrender.

'No disrespect to the dead, but I don't suppose you can claim that we really *knew* Sebastian,' Dot said in her usual brusque fashion, her short helmet of grey hair gleaming under the overhead lights as she leaned over to pass Paula's home-made mint sauce to Dave. 'I mean, think of it—a week a year for five years is only five weeks out of nearly three hundred. For the other two hundred-odd weeks he could have been an axe-murderer for all we knew.' Dot had been too strong-minded and opinionated to get along well with Sebastian.

'Dot! Sebastian was a *doctor*!' Paula cried.

'So was Crippen,' Rafe pointed out drily.

'Rafe!' Paula reproached him with a reluctant smile.

'Who was Crippen?' asked Celia, whose blank, fresh-scrubbed face showed her lack of years as well as her lack of knowledge of forensic history.

'He was famous as the first criminal to be caught by police using a radio-telegraph,' supplied Rafe. 'Hanged in 1910 for poisoning his wife. No, you're right, Paula, I guess there's no similarity—Sebastian's method of getting rid of his wives was strictly legal. Divorce may be more expensive than murder when you're wealthy, but it's a lot less risky in the long run.'

Celia looked intrigued at the mention of wealth. 'How many wives did your father have?'

'Let's see…' From the corner of her eye Jennifer was

infuriated to see him pretend to count on his fingers, knowing he was deliberately tormenting her when he suddenly shook his head and started counting all over again.

'Four,' Jennifer interrupted flatly, deciding to take a leaf out of Rafe's book and mislead with the literal truth. 'He was divorced four times.'

'No kidding!' Dave and Celia exchanged looks, and Jennifer could see them wondering, from the supreme confidence of their youth, how anyone could screw up that many marriages.

With a pang she wondered whether, if her engagement hadn't collapsed under the weight of her brother's death and her mother's long convalescence, she and Michael mightn't have been divorced by now, too. She had loved him, and had passionately committed herself to the belief that their love would last a lifetime, but Michael's feelings had withered in the face of early adversity, leaving her nothing but false dreams and empty hopes.

'What's it like having that many mothers?' Celia wondered, her journalistic curiosity tweaked.

Jennifer went cold as she realised what could happen if Celia got wind of the bizarre story that was happening right under her very nose. Would she be able to resist the lure of another profitable scoop?

'TEST TUBE FATHER IS STEPBROTHER OF HIS OWN CHILD!'

It was the kind of story that tabloids and talk shows could play up for weeks—years, even. The second most precious gift that Sebastian had given Jennifer, after her baby, had been privacy, but that would be well and truly blasted into smithereens if anyone in the media got hold of the details.

Rafe didn't seem to find Celia's question intrusive, but then he asked some unnervingly intrusive questions himself.

'My own mother divorced Sebastian when I was four, and he didn't marry for the second time until I was in my teens, by which time I'd long since lost the desire to regard any of his changing guard of consorts in a maternal light.' He gave a quick glance at Jennifer that brought a little sting to her cheek. 'Fortunately for me, as it turned out, because all *their* motherly instincts were already focused on their own children.'

There was a neutrality in his voice that spoke volumes to Jennifer.

'So were you brought up by your mother or Sebastian?' wondered Paula.

Jennifer's eyes lowered to her plate as she tried to conceal her interest in his reply. Although Sebastian had often spoken about his son, it had usually been in the form of some grudging boast of his achievements, or a complaint about Rafe's refusal to show proper filial respect. Suddenly she wanted the knowledge she had previously rejected. While the father of her child had been anonymous it hadn't mattered, but now that he had become a force in her life she needed to know the things that had shaped his personality, if only to enable her to correspondingly shape her defences.

'My mother, thank goodness—she's Italian and has very firm feelings about mother-son bonding.' Without looking at him, Jennifer knew he was smiling. 'My father, on the other hand, worked hard and he played hard. He liked to bask in the image of himself as a family man, but the reality was that he couldn't hack the boring, everyday routines of parenthood. He couldn't be bothered with children until they became old enough to behave like real people. He liked the world ordered to his own liking, and children, of course, are notoriously allergic to order...'

A distant low boom made them all look towards the window, where the brooding hulk of volcanic rock and ice that was Ruapehu was still just barely visible against the spreading inky stain of night. A little earlier the thick mushroom cloud of ash and steam haloing the summit had looked like boiling red dye, the falling particles of ash absorbing the refracted rays of the setting sun and diffusing them into a brilliant red-orange haze that had made the whole mountain look as if it had caught fire, the permanent ice on the highest ridges blushing a fluorescent orange-pink while the lower snow-clad slopes dropped away into deep violet-blue shadows.

Another faraway crack and Dave, who had busied his mouth with food rather than conversation, pushed his plate away, wiping his beard with his napkin as he jumped to his feet, crackling with energy.

'I think that's our cue. They must be pretty huge blasts if we can hear them all the way down here. I hope you don't mind if we take off.'

'We have no idea what time we'll be back,' said Celia, running a hand through her bubbly blonde hair. 'I mean, it depends on what's happening out there...'

'We'll leave the key in the front door for you,' said Jennifer, smiling up at them. 'So you won't have to worry about waking us up when you come in.'

Rafe looked startled at the suggestion. 'Isn't that a bit risky?' he asked as the couple departed. 'Leaving the place unlocked at night.'

'This isn't London,' Jennifer told him with a superior sniff. 'We're a small community; we prefer to trust people to behave decently rather than to live in a perpetual state of siege against potential muggers and burglars.'

'I'd like to trust people too, but experience has taught me that it's painfully unwise.'

Jennifer would have liked to argue against his cynicism, but she was hardly in a position to talk to him about trust.

'Of course, in the season, when there's a big influx of

tourists, we do get an increase in petty crime and vandalism, that kind of thing,' Paula chipped in. 'But being a little off the beaten track, as we are here, we don't worry about it. Why, when we first moved in we didn't even have a lock on the door!'

That led to a discussion about the origins of Beech House, a blessedly safe topic as far as Jennifer was concerned, and she happily left the three of them talking as she cleared away the plates and went to fetch the rhubarb pie from the oven.

But when she came back the conversation had turned to the renovations that had been carried out over the past three years, and how Jennifer had been so clever at handling the business side of things that she had recently been able to pay off the substantial mortgage and medical bills, and take out medical insurance that covered one hundred per cent of any care that Paula might require, so that she wouldn't have to be reliant on the badly overstretched public hospital system.

Jennifer pushed rhubarb pie and cream at her mother to try and stop her singing her paean to the wonderful, supportive daughter she had, but Paula refused to be diverted.

'She probably didn't tell you because she tends to hide her light under a bushel, but after the accident life was such a struggle for the two of us. We had managed to scrape enough to put a deposit on this house, but there was nothing left over and Jenny had to give up her nurse's training to care for me. Once I was a bit more mobile she got several part-time home-caring jobs, then decided to start the bed and breakfast for the extra income. But I think that was mostly for me at first, wasn't it, Jenny? She was desperate to jolt me out of my depression and get me interested and involved in life again. Pain does tend to turn one in on oneself terribly...

'Anyway, then Dot came along and decided she

wanted to more or less have her room permanently, and she started doing the grounds—' she gave her friend a beam '—and I started giving some cooking classes, and soon we had so many regular guests that Jenny was able to give up her other jobs and run Beech House in a more businesslike way, so that she could borrow the money to invest in the renovations. I insisted one of the first things she do was expand that attic of hers so she had some more space for herself, and somewhere to do her paperwork. She's so meticulous about her records and files, she spends hours up there most nights, tapping away at that computer...'

'Girl's a genius with money—seems to be able to stretch it like rubber,' said Dot, cutting herself another fat slice of rhubarb pie. 'Of course, thrift is a forgotten art to most people these days, and someone like you probably never had to learn it—'

'Oh, I know the value of a pound,' said Rafe drily. He also knew something about business and building costs, and his shrewd eye had estimated that tens of thousands of dollars must have gone into the remodelling of Beech House...a great deal more money than any bank would have been justified in loaning to such a small-scale business. Jennifer wasn't just a genius, she was a magician, and Rafe had a burning ambition to discover the source of her mysterious magic.

'I may have had what you would class as a privileged childhood, but I worked for my own living from the time I was seventeen,' he told Paula and Dot, bemused by his nagging desire to make a good impression, even though he knew that by the time he left the two women would probably have every reason to despise him. 'My father offered to pay me an allowance if I went to medical school, but I chose art school instead and dropped out of that when modelling turned out to be so lucrative. Apart from what I inherited a few months ago, everything I have I earned through my own blood, sweat and fears!'

'You mean tears.' Jennifer was unable to resist correcting the misquoted cliché.

He turned his head, the skin slanting over his high cheekbones as he smiled. 'I mean that without any business training, every time I expanded into some new venture it was hands-on, trial and error stuff that had a huge potential for disaster—I take on small failing enterprises and turn them around; that's nail-biting stuff.'

'So you're an entrepreneur,' said Dot, pleased to have discovered where he fitted in the scheme of things. 'You take the initiative, you take the risk, and then you sell and take the profit.'

'Oh, I don't sell,' said Rafe. 'I keep. When I make a success of something, I'm possessive. I do what I do for *me*, and I pick and choose my targets because they interest me, not just for their profit potential. Maybe I should hire *you* to work for me,' he aimed across Jennifer's bows. 'Then you could teach my accountants some of that incredible thrift...'

'You're the *last* person I'd ever work for,' she said hotly, before remembering their audience.

'You don't believe in husbands and wives working together?' Rafe smoothly covered her gaffe.

'Uh, n-no, I think it's asking for t-trouble,' she stammered.

'God forbid we do that!' he murmured, his green eyes declaring that they had plenty enough of that already.

'Your father and I worked together for twenty-five years in perfect harmony,' protested Paula. 'Though I admit we weren't shut up in an office together, and of course he was the one with the real job while I was an unpaid accessory, but still, I was pretty essential to his ministry.'

'I should imagine you made a wonderful vicar's wife,'

said Rafe, with a frank sincerity that made Paula pinken in pleasure. 'I don't really work in an office, either. It's more a case of have laptop will travel, because I like to keep a close eye on my favourite projects. I have a company that handles personal management for celebrities, several art galleries, a theatre production company, a few publishing ventures—'

'Publishing?' Dot's broad forehead creased with interest.

'Oh, Jenny, you made Rafe sound like a boring businessman when you said what he did, but now I know why you two felt such an instant affinity. Jenny is an inveterate reader and loves to write!' Her mother clapped her hands together.

'The reading I know about—but, writing?' Rafe's golden eyebrows rose at Jennifer's trapped expression.

'Just a hobby,' she said quickly, aghast. 'Dot's the one who's the writer...'

After a thoughtful hesitation, Rafe's gaze was reluctantly diverted. 'Oh, what are you doing, Dot?'

The older woman waved a dismissive hand. 'Been doing it for years. Travel book...all the places I've been...personal journey, that kind of thing. I'm not in any hurry to finish it, though—I haven't done all my travelling yet!'

'There's a big market for travel books,' Rafe said, and he and Dot proceeded to pick apart some of the offerings they had read in common.

Rafe cleverly lured Jennifer into the discussion as the talk broadened into books and writing in general, and by the time they moved into the living room with their tea and coffee she had forgotten her agonised self-consciousness, forgotten to guard and examine every word before she uttered it and was arguing as warmly as the other two, her body relaxed yet simmering with vitality, her brown eyes glowing with passion, her capable hands darting to illustrate her words.

She didn't even care that she had to sit close to Rafe on the couch to satisfy her mother's expectation of marital bliss. No longer stiff and repressed, she flowered under the fierce cut and thrust of ideas, her animation flowing like wine through her veins, bringing a luminous warmth to her pale features and softening the square of her face as she ardently defended her point of view with wit and humour.

Although Jennifer loved Paula and Dot, and had planned to be utterly content with her future at Beech House, the strange double life she lived—of wild, passionate flights of daring imagination on the one hand and intensely practical, down-to-earth respectability on the other—had its drawbacks. She maintained a careful separation of the two starkly opposing sides of her personality, and at the moment they were revelling in their unexpected outing together!

Only when her mother mentioned that Jennifer had once taken some creative writing courses did the barriers slam back into place.

'Sebastian was very intrigued—wasn't he, Jenny?— that first time he stayed here.' Paula laughed. 'He found a scrap of something you'd written and you were horribly mortified when he said he'd read it and thought it was good. I remember how amused he was when you came over all shy, Jenny, and blushed like a tomato when he tried to talk to you about it. She hates people to read what she's done,' she confided, to Rafe's intense interest. 'I think that was why she was so keen on getting a computer for the bookings and accounts, so she can write to her heart's content without leaving embarrassing scraps of paper floating about for all and sundry to see.'

'Because it's just private scribblings,' said Jenny desperately, feeling her colour inexorably rising. It would be her mother who would die of mortification if she ever found out exactly what it was that her daughter was writing, and how sinfully successful she was at it!

She got up to take a jab at the cheerfully blazing logs on the fire with the cast-iron poker, hoping her blush would be put down to her proximity to the heat. The way Rafe was looking at her she felt as if the guilty truth was written in scarlet letters on her forehead.

'What sort of things do your companies publish, Rafe?' she heard Dot say as she pretended to be engrossed in the sparks that were flying off the blackened surface of the logs.

'Oh, there's a couple of high-class fashion magazines, and one or two aimed at, uh, the sophisticated male...' Jennifer smiled maliciously to herself at his revealing euphemism. 'Then I have one publishing house that specialises in children's books and another that prints general and genre fiction. I also have a couple of niche publishers under the wing of a company I bought a majority interest in from my father a few years ago, after he'd rescued it from one of my stepbrothers, who'd driven it to the verge of bankruptcy with his incompetent management. One produces medical text and reference books and the other publishes series fiction for women.'

'What kind of women's fiction?' Paula asked, having become an avid reader of wrenching emotional sagas during her convalescence. 'Do you have any famous female authors?'

'Not famous outside their narrow field, no. As I said, it's a niche market. I guess you could say that Velvet Books are sort of educational—'

There was a sharp clang as Jennifer dropped the heavy poker on the hearth, nearly impaling her foot with its viciously barbed end.

She stared at Rafe in glassy-eyed horror.

Velvet?

Rafe owned the English company that was fast becoming the leading international publisher of female erotica? *He* was behind those elegantly sexy paperbacks which had tapped into the gap in the market between steamy sensual romances and crudely sexual romps?

The whole picture suddenly leapt into ghastly focus in her head—Sebastian's vague publishing 'contact' all those years ago had been a member of his own family!

She felt a hot burst of maniacal laughter building up inside her.

Velvet novels were a lot of things: sinfully smouldering, intensely exciting, wildly romantic and exquisitely erotic.

But 'sort of educational'?

Jennifer put a hand over her mouth to hold in her hysterical giggle.

Rafe had sprung up, misunderstanding her horror, sliding his cupped hands supportively under her elbows as she swayed in front of the fire.

'Jennifer? Are you all right? Did you hurt yourself?' he murmured into her owl-eyed confusion. When she didn't immediately answer he knelt to run his hands over her feet, assuring himself that they were undamaged.

She blinked back to life, staring down at his blond head, conscious of how close she'd come to needlessly giving herself away. Thank God she'd never used her own name, not even in the earliest correspondence. She would never have even considered taking Sebastian's advice if she hadn't been able to wrap herself in complete anonymity. Only her lawyer and the tax department were aware that she was two people.

Certainly not the man kneeling at her feet.

Like a pleading supplicant, she thought, and felt another dangerous bubble of laughter form as she contemplated the awful irony of the situation.

'I'm s-sorry. Uh—it was just the shock,' she said with

perfect truth, regretting it when he rose, regarding her with a glimmer of suspicion.

'It slipped out of my hand,' she added, laying it on. 'I nearly spiked myself.'

He pushed her gently back towards the couch before bending to pick up the fallen poker, weighing it for a moment in his grip before dropping it back into its guard.

Bonzer, who was sprawled on the sheepskin hearthrug, lifted his head for a throaty growl as Rafe moved past his line of vision.

'Pipe down, Bonzer!' said Dot, tossing him an after-dinner mint which he snapped up not at all lazily.

'Sharp reflexes, old man,' said Rafe, crouching to give the dog a pat and a lazy scratch on his tubby belly. Bonzer whined and squirmed with delight, his tail thumping against the rug.

'How long have you had him?' Rafe asked Jennifer.

She had almost recovered her equilibrium. 'Three years. I found him out on the road in a ditch. He'd been hit by a car and had a broken hip, and for a while the vet thought he might have to put him down. But he got better and nobody claimed him, so I brought him home. I think he was about four when we got him, and obviously nobody had ever tried to train him so he didn't take to discipline too well. He's still a bit boisterous and dopey, but he's very friendly and he loves children...'

She had said the words without thinking, but when Rafe looked up at her she had a vision of a little green-eyed, golden-skinned, tow-headed boy, shouting with laughter as he had his face licked by his doggy friend. Her lips curved dreamily, unconsciously inviting him to share in her fantasy, and Rafe's pupils expanded, darkening his eyes to a moody jade as he stared with a peculiar kind of hunger at her tender expression of delight. The delicate silence lasted until Rafe looked away and caught sight of Maxie, sharpening his claws against the logs in the basket.

'And what about your cats, are they former strays too?'

'How did you guess?' grinned Paula. 'And Fergus.' She pointed at the cage in the corner where an overly plump budgie listed drunkenly on a perch. With an incredulous look at Jennifer, Rafe scrambled up to take a closer look.

'Good God, that's why it's on a slant.' Rafe peered into the cage. 'It's only got one leg!'

'But, as Jenny pointed out to the vet, it's a very *sturdy* leg,' laughed Dot.

Jenny braced herself for more jokes about her rescued menagerie, but Ruapehu had a more dramatic subject in mind.

A low roar and a series of deep sonic booms had them rushing for the verandah, standing spellbound in the freezing night air at the sight of the incandescent fireworks spitting arcing streamers of molten fire hundreds of metres above the mountain crater. Even knowing that they were at a safe distance, Jennifer shuddered at the awe-inspiring, raw power unleashed by the volcano. She felt like a small, lonely, insignificant dot in a vast universe, and welcomed the strong arms that closed about her, pulling her back against the warm, solid body of another human being.

'Now I know why Dante calls nature "the art of God",' said Rafe quietly over the top of her head, his words forming as steam in the icy air, his arms tightening around her waist. 'Magnificent and terrifying, and powerful beyond our comprehension.'

It was hypnotically fascinating watching the fiery jets of super-heated liquid rock, propelled by the violent eruption of gases, fountain continuously over the rocky outline of the cone. Huge, flaming orange 'bombs' were flung out amongst the cascading rivulets of white-hot fire, and through Dot's binoculars some could be seen tumbling and melting down the snowy west face of the mountain like giant fluorescent tears. Dark ash blotted out more of the stars as it streamed up into the atmosphere, creating a huge black void above the brilliant pyrotechnic display.

Eventually it was the cold that drove them back inside, and while Dot and her mother elected to stay in the living room, wrapped in blankets with hot toddies on their knees, to watch the continuing fireworks as long as they could manage to stay awake, a few yawns and coy hints from Rafe had led to Jennifer being shooed upstairs to bed for the sake of her ostensibly tired 'husband'.

As she'd suspected, when they got up to her room Rafe's tiredness miraculously fell away, as did the cloak of relatively civilised restraint he had worn in company. He was back to the restless, hostile, suspicious and openly aggressive enemy he had been on his arrival. Only now there was an added element, a primitive possessiveness in his insulting gaze that made her spine crawl with apprehensive excitement.

He watched calmly, arms folded across his black chest, as she busily folded spare double blankets from the glory box at the foot of the bed to form a narrow mattress on the floor and covered it with a thick quilt, tucking a fat pillow at the head.

Then, just as calmly, he stalked over and tore her work apart, tossing the blankets and quilt in opposite directions and kicking the pillow under the bed.

'You're not doing me out of my feather bed,' he told her, his body language spoiling for a fight—legs astride, hands on hips, shoulders tense, stubborn jaw thrust slightly forward.

Laboriously, silently, Jennifer collected all the discarded pieces and constructed the makeshift bed all over again.

'This is for *me*, not for *you*,' she announced haughtily, completing her statement by ramming the pillow back into position. It galled her, but she knew she didn't have a hope in hell of keeping him out of the big bed, if that was where he wanted to be.

He grunted and pulled off his shoes, not the laced walking boots this time, she noticed, but elegant, black, hand-made Italian jobs. Any moment now he would start the strip, and Jennifer was not going to be put through *that* humiliation again!

She hurried over to her nightwear drawer and blindly grabbed a handful of garments. Then she slammed into the bathroom and locked the door. Maybe if she took an age to shower and clean her teeth and brush her hair and—and...hell, and give herself a manicure, pedicure, perm, the whole works!—maybe by then he would be harmlessly asleep.

He'd better be asleep, she groaned silently as she looked at her choice of sleepwear. Of course there was no prim flannel nightdress or practical passion-killing pyjamas. She didn't own any. Although Jennifer plumped for comfort over fashion in her clothes, her underwear was a different matter. There she felt free to indulge her private fantasies, and sexy bits of nothing featured large in her lingerie drawers. As for the slinky, sensuous things she slept in—they were intended to inspire the kind of wicked dreams that swept her to fresh heights of passionate creativity!

With Raphael Jordan in her bed, she needed a soporific, not an aphrodisiac!

CHAPTER SIX

MUFFLED up in the old pink towelling bathrobe that she never used, Jennifer crept past the sunken lump in the bed. Rafe had turned off the overhead lights and only the lamp beside the bed shone, throwing a rich glow over the golden head on the pillow. He was lying on his stomach, face half buried to one side in the pillow, one smooth-muscled naked arm thrown up around his head as if to shield himself from the intrusive light.

Jennifer glided across the cool floorboards, the shivery thrills goosing over her skin having nothing to do with the temperature. In fact the room, well-insulated in walls and ceiling, was quite toasty warm, thanks to the thermostatically controlled convection heater in the corner.

The hush of the night was disturbed by the muffled crump of faraway explosion, and she was irresistibly drawn to the balcony doors for another look at the fireworks display. After nearly two hours the powerful forces were showing no sign of diminishing, and now lightning bolts were crackling around the summit, threading zig-zag patterns of brilliant white through the black ash-clouds roaring into the night sky.

'You're blocking the view.'

She turned quickly, almost tripping over the drooping hem of her robe. The first thing she saw was Rafe propped up on his elbow, the cream duvet sliding away from his bare chest to settle at his waist.

The second was that her meagre bed on the floor had vanished. And this time there were no scattered bedclothes or assaulted pillow.

'I thought you were asleep.'

He made a negative movement with his head, abrading his whiskers against the knuckles that were propping up his jaw as he contemplated her deep dismay.

'Did you really think I was going to make it that easy for you?' he said, with menacingly softness.

Easy?

Jennifer had no illusions on that score. But she *had* hoped to put off another devastating confrontation until she had had time to repair the weaknesses in her buckled defences, particularly in view of this wretched new complication. She just hoped to God that Rafe wasn't involved in the editorial side of Velvet Books!

She ignored his taunting reply and flung open the glory box. It was empty. With a furious glance at Rafe's innocent expression her gaze hunted around the room for the missing blankets.

'This is just childish!' she burst out.

'I agree, so stop behaving like a sulky schoolgirl. Come to bed and we'll talk about it like mature adults. You know what they say—a husband and wife should never let the sun go down on their anger...'

She let the lid of the box fall with a sharp crack that echoed her snapping nerves.

'We are *not* married and I'm *not* getting into bed with you!'

'Claiming the moral high ground? That's pretty shaky territory for a compulsive liar...'

'*You* can talk about morality?' she scorned fiercely. 'You've had more women than you've had hot dinners!'

His mouth took on a cynical slant. 'I presume you got that spicy tidbit from my father. Well, maybe that's what I wanted him to think, when rebelling against his hypocritical version of morality was my chief aim in life, but in fact I've always been extremely selective where women are concerned—certainly more sexually discriminating than *he* ever was. Sebastian was congenitally

incapable of being faithful to one women, yet he per-
sisted in making vows of fidelity, while I, on the other
hand, never made any promises and never once betrayed
a lover.'

'I'm not in the least interested in your sex life,'
Jennifer bit out.

'Yes, you are. Or you wouldn't constantly stroke me
with those hot little looks from under your lashes.'

She immediately flashed her eyes wide. 'I do not!'

'Did you think I hadn't noticed? I spent a good few
years in front of the camera, learning how to attract that
particular look from women—I know exactly what it
signals. There was never any hint of sexual awareness
in the air between you and my father, but you and I...we
were a different story, weren't we?' His voice deepened
as his eyes swept her from head to foot, mocking her
scruffy armour. 'Even if we chose not to acknowledge
it, that delicious sting of mutual curiosity was always
there, wasn't it? You might even say that the atmosphere
between us was pregnant with possibilities...although at
the time I didn't realise how literally true that would
turn out to be!'

Jennifer yanked the belt on her robe cuttingly tight,
trying to separate herself from the wicked sensations
shimmering through her lower body as Rafe rolled onto
his back, exposing more of his torso, folding his arms
provocatively behind his head as he said boldly, 'You
know, at one stage it did occur to me that I could seduce
you away from Sebastian, but then I figured, Why should
I do the three witches' dirty work for them...?'

He meant Lydia, Sharon and Felicity, the bitchy tri-
umvirate who, unlike Rafe's mother, had remained
firmly within Sebastian's orbit, playing on his spasmodic
guilt and pandering to his obsession that they should all
be one, big happy family. Sebastian's regrettable habit
of throwing money at problems to make them go away

had only served to multiply the problems of his ex-wives and their children.

'Besides, the old man was dying—all his riches couldn't protect him from that—so why shouldn't he spend them going out with a bang, so to speak, rather than a whimper?' Rafe continued, with an insultingly careless tilt of one gilded shoulder. 'So I resisted the temptation to respond to your subtle invitation—'

'There *was* no invitation!' she hissed, stooping to peer under the bed. 'Where have you put my damned blankets?'

'I threw them off the balcony.'

She popped up again, her face furiously flushed.

'You didn't!' she gasped, clutching her lapels, imagining what her mother and Dot must have thought when bedclothes had suddenly come raining down in front of their eyes.

'For a consummate liar you're incredibly gullible yourself,' he jeered. 'No, I didn't—but even if you find them it's not going to get you anywhere. I'm not going to let you sleep on the floor. Apart from anything else it won't do the baby any good...'

'What the hell do you care?' she snarled unwisely, recoiling from any hint of potential interest in her pregnancy.

His eyes narrowed as he sensed her fear. 'Why don't you come over here and find out?' he invited, with silken insolence. 'You might be surprised to find what we care about in common...'

Her heart jittered. Oh, no, she wasn't falling for that one. She wasn't going to get within striking distance of that lithe golden body. As long as he didn't touch her she could maintain her defiant front.

She tossed her head in an unconsciously challenging gesture of contempt. 'Forget it!' she said, flouncing over to the door. 'The Carters' room is empty tonight, I can sleep downstairs in *their* bed.'

Braced for an explosion of thwarted anger she was disconcerted when he remained relaxed against the pillows, a look of boredom on his face.

She soon found out why when the door refused to open to her touch. She rattled the handle in frustration, realised what was wrong and whirled around.

'What have you done with the key?'

He unfolded his arms and spread them wide, boredom replaced by a smug smile. 'I'll give you a clue. It's somewhere in this bed. Why don't you feel around and I'll let you know when you're getting warm?'

She was very warm now, and getting hotter by the moment. If only she could *melt* through the door at her back. 'You're the most hateful person I've ever met!' she dredged from the depths of her helplessness.

His smile vanished. 'If that's the way you feel, maybe I'm right to worry about how carefully you're looking after your pregnancy. Have you changed your mind about having my hateful baby? Are you hoping your body might reject it?'

Jennifer was stricken to the core. 'That's a vicious thing to say,' she choked, welcoming the pain of her shoulderblades digging into the door as a distraction from the searing pain in her heart. 'I'd *never* hurt my baby! And I'd never blame an innocent child for the acts of its parents, either. Children don't have any choice about who their parents are going to be—'

'And parenthood often isn't a matter of conscious choice either, but it was for *you*,' he pointed out ruthlessly. 'On the day you agreed to be inseminated with my sperm you made a choice. You accepted Raphael Jordan as the father of your child. You accepted me!

'Now, are you going to come over here and get into bed or do I have to come over there and fetch you?'

He sat up and began to peel down the duvet, revealing more and more naked flesh.

Jennifer squeezed her eyes tight shut against the threatening sight, throwing up her hands to ward off her invisible panic. 'No, wait. Look, can't we just…?'

She heard the rustle of sheets, his bare feet hitting the floor, his quiet padding across the room towards her. And then nothing. Silence.

She swallowed, her nostrils quivering at the scent of danger. He was close, standing directly in front of her; she could feel his proximity with every nerve in her body. Her imagination went into overdrive. If she moved her hands even a fraction of an inch she would touch his hot, smooth, satiny skin…

'You can look now.'

The sardonic humour in his voice warned her to ignore him.

She licked her dry lips and was ashamed of the slight whimper that slipped out. 'Please…'

He took her resistant left hand and placed it on his hip. Her eyes flew open and she looked down in blessed relief. He was wearing a pair of black silk pyjama trousers, loosely tied by a drawstring. They had settled low on his lean hips, dipping on his hard belly at the point where the arrow of hair below his navel began to spread into a dark blond thicket. But at least he was respectably covered.

She snatched her gaze back to his face. It was all hard angles and brooding shadows, his lower lip pushed out in a sombre, sexy pout.

'Disappointed?' he smouldered, and massaged her hand in slow circles on the fabric, shaping her palm over the jutting hardness of his hip-bone.

There was another electric silence, and he picked up her right hand and put it on his right hip. Then he re-

moved her spectacles, folded them, and tucked them
snugly into the breast pocket of her robe.

'Wh-why did you do that?' she said light-headedly,
as he withdrew his fingers from the pocket, his knuckles
scraping briefly against her towelling-padded breast.

'You won't need your glasses in bed. Everything you
see there is going to be in close-up,' he murmured, his
forehead briefly resting against hers as he looked down
for the belt of her robe. 'You won't need this, either.'

'Don't...' she uttered weakly, stopping him, her toes
curling against the bare floorboards.

'You won't be comfortable all bundled up like this.'
He tugged gently at the trailing bow.

She tipped up her face to protest and, shockingly, her
mouth met his. His lips were firm and resilient, his
tongue limber as it slipped moistly past the guard of her
teeth and stroked her silky interior. Shock turned to violent craving and she moaned, her mouth opening to receive him. His head tilted, his mouth slanting to deepen
the kiss, deepen the penetration of his tongue into her
willing depths. He broke off and bit at her lips, licking
and sucking at the juicy pink flesh, his hands twisting in
the loops of her belt, dragging her closer into the hot,
wet embrace of mouths.

His whiskers rasped on her delicate skin, the small
pain intensifying the oral pleasure as she savaged him
in return, and he groaned, plunging himself even more
recklessly into her inviting moistness, the ragged sound
of his desire vibrating seductively in her arching throat.
His tongue flickered over hers in a dance of erotic com-
pulsion, rubbing at her, teasing her with addictive skill,
saturating her overloaded senses with his unique taste.

Her body tightened, her breasts swelling against the
rough towelling as he seduced her tongue into his mouth
so that he could suckle her in a slow, hard rhythm that
matched the sensual undulation of his hips.

Only when she felt his hands move at her waist, fumbling again with the now impossibly knotted belt, did Jennifer drag herself back from the brink of terrifying surrender.

'No, oh, no, we can't...' She tore her mouth from his, the words breaking clumsily from swollen lips, her tortured lungs struggling for the breath he had stolen.

'Can't what?' he muttered, his mouth seeking across her averted cheek, his voice richly clotted with passion.

She had to force herself to think logically. 'Can't—can't go to bed together...' She groaned. That was where they were headed, wasn't it?

He raised his head. His eyes, sultry and heavy-lidded, were glittering slits of molten green. 'Why not? It's what we both want.' His voice roughened to a guttural scrawl. 'And there's nothing to stop us any more...'

Why not? The words whispered seductively in her brain. Why not take what you want...and pay for it?

But no, not like this. It was too dangerous, the gamble too great, the stakes too high.

'We just *can't*...' she whispered.

There was a heartbeat's pause before he responded, brushing his mouth across her feathery fringe. 'Would you do it if I paid you?' he urged softly, the golden shadow of his beard capturing several strands of her hair, sliding them across his mouth as he turned his face to breathe his sin against her temple. 'Would you strip for me if I gave you money, darling? Would you take off your clothes, slowly...and touch yourself for me?' His creamy voice curdled into brutal cynicism as he went relentlessly on. 'How much for your body, Jennifer? How much would it cost me to do whatever the hell I liked with it? How much do you charge to have a man's stolen sperm planted inside you?'

By the time he had uttered the last bitter word he had her thrust against the wood, his hands trapping her shoulders, his thigh pressing across her legs, his searing questions battering at her horrified emotions.

'It wasn't *stolen*; you *donated* it,' she protested wildly, pushing at his bulging biceps as she fought an avalanche of undeserved guilt. She wasn't going to be blamed for *his* mistakes as well as her own. 'You went there voluntarily—you said so yourself—and you weren't at all bothered about the consequences *then*. You didn't care about any potential babies *then*. All you cared about was getting back at your father! It was *your* idea, so if there's any blaming to be done you have to take a fair share for yourself.'

'Anonymity was intrinsic to the whole process,' he tore at her savagely. 'And if my sperm wasn't stolen then why is it I feel *raped*?'

Jennifer went slack against the door, her defensive anger shattered by his tormented bewilderment. Her fingers relaxed on his straining muscles, and she began unconsciously soothing him with tiny movements of her fingertips. Her mind reeled at the knowledge that her selfish attempts to protect herself had caused him such pain. She couldn't bear it.

'No, oh, no, no, no...' She shook her head, the bluntcut ends of her hair fluttering across his white knuckles. Her eyes were dark with empathy. 'Please don't say that, don't even *think* it; it's not that way at all—'

'No? So tell me the way it is, Jennifer,' he said harshly. 'Make me feel less violated. Tell me how a woman who makes a living out of caring for other people, who sacrifices her career for her disabled mother, who spends her own money building up a business so two old people will feel secure and needed, who's a sucker for a wounded stray...tell me how a woman like that could knowingly exploit a sick old man's obsession for what she could get out of it. Did the money really mean that much to you?'

It was the 'knowingly' that did it. Jennifer's own sick sense of betrayal came rushing back.

'*Will you stop talking about the money?*' she said fiercely. '*Yes*, Sebastian gave me a marriage settlement, and, *yes*, I took it. But I *didn't do it for the money.*'

'Then in God's name *why*?' He shook her shoulders in a violent fit of frustration. 'What else did you hope to gain from it? His name? His power?'

He was so smart, yet he still couldn't see it! Because it hadn't mattered at all to him, while to her it was *everything*.

'A *baby*!' She yelled her contempt for his blind stupidity. '*That's* what I had to gain! I made a bargain to marry Sebastian because I wanted to have a baby!'

His hands fell away. He looked utterly thunderstruck, and, perversely, that gave her the courage to carry on.

'I did it to have a baby,' she admitted painfully, crossing her arms under her breasts. 'All right? I did it because I wanted a baby of my own and Sebastian promised to give me one if I helped him secure the trust against the witches.'

She saw his expression change from one of stunned incomprehension to raging incredulity. Next, she was certain, would be disgust.

'Well, what was I *supposed* to do?' she cried. 'I'm twenty-seven, single, not in a relationship—not even *interested* in getting married....there was no way I was going to get pregnant naturally, unless I was willing to pick up a man just for sex...and I didn't want my baby to be born out of some sordid liaison that I would be ashamed of—not to mention the risks of doing something like that. But I did want a child of my own so much...'

She turned her face aside so that he wouldn't see the sheen in her eyes as she remembered her fierce yearning for a dream that had seemed to be slipping further and

further out of her reach. A hand under her chin forced
her to look back at him. The humiliating look of disbelief had gone from his eyes, but it wasn't disgust that
she saw in its place; it was a dawning wonderment.

'Th-then Sebastian came back to stay,' she said huskily. 'And it seemed natural to talk about it with him—
he'd spent his life helping people to have children. We
talked about options, and then he told me about his pros-
tate cancer, and said we could help each other. He…he
offered a way for me to get pregnant that would be completely clinical and safe…and free. It was like a miracle.
All I had to do was have my doctor do some tests, accompany him to England…a-and marry him—'

'All…?' Rafe's hand smoothed her towelling lapel,
creased by her anxious kneading.

She flushed at his sarcasm. 'It was so that Felicity
wouldn't get her hands on the trust,' she said flatly. 'He
said there was a loophole, that she'd be able take over
as trustee when he died, or before that if he got very ill
and was judged incompetent, because she was his most
recent wife.'

Rafe opened his mouth as if to protest, then closed it
again, and after a brief hesitation said drily, 'He must
have trusted you to the hilt.'

'He knew I only cared about the baby,' Jennifer said
with touching naïveté. 'Under our bargain we *both* got
what we most wanted—I had my baby and he got my
name on all his legal documents…'

'And a grandchild to bear his name,' he reminded her
heavily. 'So it never made you feel queasy that it was
my baby he was bargaining with? You never wondered
if maybe *I* had a right to know he was putting his grandchild into your womb…'

She whirled away towards the windows, putting her
hands to her hot cheeks.

Tell him.

He knew his father, knew the lengths he'd been willing to go to get his own way. Why should she protect Sebastian any longer when he hadn't protected *her*?

Tell him.

She could feel Rafe on her heels, pursuing her for an answer, but she couldn't turn, couldn't face him.

'It wasn't supposed to be yours,' she whispered wretchedly.

'What?' He circled in front of her, catching her by the sleeve. '*What* did you say?'

But she didn't have to repeat it. He stared at her anguished embarrassment, the echo of disillusionment in her shimmering eyes, and she saw it all come together in his mind, saw the precise moment when the intuitive leap of his intelligence suddenly made sense of all the confusing contradictions.

'My God...he didn't tell you,' he breathed, the realisation transformed into instant, utter certainty. He peeled her hands gently away from her scalding cheeks. 'The manipulating bastard didn't tell you that the donated sperm was mine. Did he? *Did he?*'

She shook her head, the tears that had been in abeyance for months spilling over—tears for her tarnished miracle.

'I—I didn't know whose it was; I didn't *want* to know,' she cried. 'You just fill in a questionnaire about the physical characteristics you'd like the father to have...I did put down tall and blond, and—but I never— it wasn't... He didn't tell me until that awful afternoon at the hospital, the day he died.' Another sob tore from her aching chest. 'He...he s-said that he'd been wrong not to tell me from the beginning, but that it didn't change our bargain, it didn't have to matter... But it did, oh, *it did!*'

She closed her eyes in memory of the devastating shock. 'I didn't know he was going to tell you as well.

I know I shouldn't have run away from the hospital like that, but, oh, God—how could I have stayed? I didn't know what to do, what to think...I felt so alone. How could he expect me to see you, to talk to you, to act naturally around you knowing...knowing that...?'

'Ah, don't, Jennifer...don't!' Rafe gathered her against his bare torso, rocking her with his strength, sinking his fingers into her soft brown hair and combing it soothingly against the back of her skull, letting her sob out her repressed anger and betrayal.

Her damp face buried in the crisp curls on his chest, her arms wrapped around his solid waist, Jennifer couldn't help but become aware of the growing tension in his body as her storm of emotion eased and he continued to stroke her back and nuzzle at her hair, murmuring nonsensical words of reassurance, acknowledging that they had both been victims of his father's hidden scheming.

He wiped her face with her towelling lapel and then proceeded to erase the evidence of her tears with kisses, his lips moving down over her tangled lashes to her pink nose and the salty traces on her cheeks. Her lips, still rosy from his previous kisses, were tasted and savoured anew.

'Rafe...'

His hand, tangled in her hair, wouldn't let her evade his sensual assault.

'Tell me what it feels like to have me inside you?' he whispered into her mouth.

She groaned.

'You love it, don't you?' He sipped the husky sound from her lips. 'In spite of everything that's happened, you love the feeling that your body is changing, ripening, stretching itself to fit around my baby...'

His long, languorous kisses and sinuous words made

her feel exquisitely feminine, earthy and voluptuously
sensual.

'Share the feeling with me, Jen. Let me make love to
the mother of my child…'

Shaken by the intensity of need in his voice, she
leaned back to look into his face and was surprised when
he instantly let her go.

She put a hand to her breast and took an uncertain
step back, her face flushed with a mingling of guilt and
desire as she realised he was giving her the freedom to
choose.

'We shouldn't…'

Rafe's body surged into full arousal as he recognised
the implicit surrender in her thready protest. The guilty
fascination with which her eyes furtively caressed him
was a fierce turn-on. It made him want to tear off her
clothes and thrust inside her without preliminaries, stak-
ing his claim and slaking his raw lust before she could
change her mind. But even stronger was his greedy desire to draw out the process of sensuous discovery as
long as possible, to spend a long time exploring, arousing, tasting, teasing…making her moan and thresh with
orgasmic pleasure before he finally granted them both
release. He wanted to be the lover she would never be
able to forget.

'You want me,' he said, deliberately thickening his
voice, permeating it with a gravelly sexuality, simultaneously both rough and smooth.

Jennifer could no longer deny it, to herself or to him,
but she found she couldn't look him in the face as she
admitted one of her most private fantasies.

She turned and looked out across the balcony, to the
mountain whose eruption symbolised the irrepressible
forces of nature. Like the force that ensured the survival
of a species, the overpowering urge of male and female
to mate, to reproduce…

'Yes. But just for tonight,' she added quickly, thinking that at least she could circumscribe her sin. Wrapped in her own doubts, she didn't consider she might be insulting his male ego.

'Just one reckless night of forbidden love,' he agreed softly, attuning himself so perfectly to her thoughts that her shoulders slumped with relief. She would not have been so relieved if she had glimpsed the grim amusement with which he had accepted her unconscious challenge

He stepped up behind her, sliding his palms from her shoulders down over her breasts to her waist.

'Shall we begin?'

In the glass doors Jennifer could see his reflection, his naked chest rising behind her shoulder, his green eyes glinting mysteriously, his hands graceful as they slowly untied her belt, knowing that this time she wasn't going to stop him.

Her robe fell open, revealing the shimmering wisp of thin forest-green silk that skimmed her body to the tops of her thighs. The shoestring straps supported a plunging scooped neckline that exposed most of the upper curves of her full breasts, the undarted bodice stretching provocatively between the two concealed peaks and then falling away to follow the indentation of her waist and smooth over her rounded hips to flirt around the V of her legs.

She found she was trembling as he looked down over her shoulder at what he had uncovered. She heard him suck in his breath at the sight of her firm creamy breasts straining against the watery silk, their faint tracery of blue veins guiding the way down to her barely concealed nipples.

'Sexy,' he growled, fingering the pure silk hem where it lay against her hip, but otherwise touching her with only his eyes as he lifted the robe from her shoulders and let it fall in a hush to the floor, leaving her exposed to his reflected view. Very exposed. She was suddenly conscious of her overripe breasts and broad hips. Her breath quickened, tugging at the silk.

'You wore this for me,' he said, still not touching her. 'You knew all along you were going to say yes...'

She licked her lips. 'No—I—all my night things are s-sexy...'

'S-sexy...' he teased, and shivers ran up and down her spine as she watched his hands come around her waist to settle on her belly and begin to inch the silk up from her thighs.

'What am I going to see next?' he whispered, nibbling at her shoulder. 'Are you wearing anything underneath this little bit of nothing?'

'Y-yes.'

'Spoilsport.'

He ravelled the silk higher with his gathering fingers and sighed when he saw the reflection of a tiny stretch-lace G-string.

'Or maybe not...' He ran his fingers down the lace edging that splayed over her hip, down between her legs to a place that made her gasp. His fingers fluttered with unbelievable delicacy against the plump folds pouting against the lace while his other hand moved up from her waist to languorously fondle her breasts, sliding beneath the silk to find her soft, velvety nipples.

'Do you like watching what I'm doing to you, darling?'

She did. It was wilder even than her reckless imagination. Fierce thrills cascaded over her in waves as she revelled in the wanton sight of the big, half-naked man standing behind his lover, his hands moving on her, pleasuring her, enslaving her with his skill.

He pulled aside her G-string and bit her ear as his fingertips teased inside her slippery heat and he whispered, 'Would you like me to take you here, like this, from behind, so that you can see it happen to you?'

Her mind exploded in a riot of sensation which had her crying out and jerking so violently that she twisted out of his grasp, surprising them both.

The fantasy interrupted, Jennifer floundered for a few breathless seconds. After what Rafe had just been doing to her she felt unbelievably, stupidly shy. She had been wildly aroused, but what about him? Wasn't she supposed to be giving *him* pleasure, too? All her stories and fantasies were conducted from the female point of view; she'd never had to consider the *man's* pleasure. And one lover followed by more than six years of celibacy hadn't exactly equipped her with confidence for the real thing!

She glanced at Rafe, to find him locked in his own world, his head tipped back and his eyes closed, his chest rising and falling as if he'd been running, his arms hanging tense at his sides, the curled fingers of one hand glistening with a faint slick of moisture that it made her blush to see it. He looked as if he was praying to some pagan god, and out in the darkness a molten fireburst accompanied by another crackle of silver brilliance seemed to be his answer.

'Oh, l-look—have you seen the lightning over the mountain...' Jennifer babbled, putting her hands against the glass doors and pushing them open. The wind must have shifted, for there was only a slight grittiness in the air as she stepped out onto the balcony. She immediately realised she was being gauche and foolish, and looked back over her shoulder. Rafe had opened his eyes and she could see the laughter in them as he slowly followed her out onto the wooden planks, but her silly nervousness vanished as she saw that, rather than mocking, his amusement was indulgent.

His thick lashes lowered and she realised he was hungrily watching the way the dark silk clung to the cheeks of her bottom as she moved and revealed flashes of the lush white globes left bare by her G-string. Feeling her confidence return in a ripple of wicked delight, she gripped the cool balcony rail and leaned forward slightly, her face still turned mischievously towards him to assess his reaction.

'Minx,' he said, studying the charmingly provocative pose with a connoisseur's approval. 'But I thought we came out here to look at a volcano erupting.'

'I'd rather watch you,' she dared confess.

'Watch me erupting?' His smile sizzled through her senses as he moved closer and cupped her downy bottom underneath the flirty hem. 'Do you want to see me lose control?' he murmured as he handled the peachy softness, tugging at the G-string to create an intimate friction between her legs.

Her fingers tightened on the rail as she unconsciously arched her back and bowed her head. 'Yes, I think I do.' She shuddered. She didn't want to be the only one…

'Then come to bed,' he purred into the nape of her neck. 'You're cold.'

She felt she would never be cool again. 'No, I'm not…'

She gasped as his hands slid up to cup her breasts, rounding them, his thumbs rubbing at her stiffened nipples.

'Then I guess you must be aroused.'

He bent his head and bit the tender curve of her neck, between nape and shoulder, his teeth grating gently against her flesh while his hands moved lazily on her breasts, his hips pushing rhythmically against the crease of her bottom, letting her feel the length of swollen shaft.

He spun her around and kissed her, hard and fast, hooking his fingers under her slender straps, pulling them sharply down her arms so that the slithery silk was dragged below her breasts, spilling their pale bounty over the shadowy fabric, an erotic contrast in colour and texture. He shaped the creamy curves and stroked the darkened tips, rolling them gently between his fingertips before bending to take them in his mouth, suckling each one in turn until they were unbearably sensitised.

His hand swept under her bottom and he lifted her in his arms, his mouth buried in hers as he carried her back inside and over to the bed, pushing her down, down, down into the feathery depths. He stripped the silk slip down over her hips and thighs and threw it off the bed, then he did the same with her G-string, his hands kneading her belly and breasts, his mouth stealing across the hidden delta of her womanhood to nuzzle into the musky darkness, his tongue lapping at the tiny budded erection there until she was racked with helpless convulsions.

Only then did he kick off his black drawstring trousers, drawing her hands down to his hugely jutting manhood, groaning thickly in ecstasy as he showed her how he liked to be touched and found her inventive enthusiasm more than he could handle and stay in control.

To Jennifer it was a dazzling revelation, beyond anything she had imagined, to have this sleek, powerful, sexy, sophisticated lover shuddering in her arms, lavishing her with his sensual praise, begging for her touch and responding to the lightest stroke of her mouth with savage abandon.

Finally he rolled over onto his back, his sweat-slicked muscles bulging as he lifted her to straddle his hips, his green eyes smouldering at her strangled cry of surprise.

'Yes…like this,' he said, his hands tightening on her hips as he teased himself against her satiny moistness. 'This way you can control how much of me you take inside you.' He gritted his teeth, finally remembering to ask, 'Is this safe?'

'If you mean will I get pregnant,' she said giddily, 'I already am.'

He shuddered, the tip of his broad shaft slipping inside her. 'No, I meant for the baby?'

'Yes, it's safe. As long as you're not too rough...' Her fingers raked through his chest hair, her hair tumbling over her feverish face as she leaned eagerly over him, her voluptuous breasts swaying towards his mouth. She wanted him and she wanted him *now*!

His eyes darkened as he eased her gently down, stretching her, sheathing himself tightly within her clinging warmth. 'I'll take good care of you, darling, I promise,' he told her. 'I'll make sure that every single orgasm is mellow and sweet and strong...'

CHAPTER SEVEN

JENNIFER stretched luxuriantly as she felt sunlight across her closed eyes, arching her back and pushing her toes towards the bottom of the bed, a delicious sense of well-being permeating her awakening body. Suspended halfway between waking and dreaming, she nestled on her side in her downy hollow, a slow smile curving her lips as she continued to drift on the lazy wings of her favourite erotic fantasy. She had Raphael Jordan at her mercy, his glorious, nude, aroused body tied to her bed, leashed for her pleasure. He was fighting against his silken bonds, his green eyes blazing fiercely as he begged—but he wasn't begging to be set free; oh, no, he wanted her to keep him, he wanted her to keep him for ever because he knew she was the only woman in the world who could satisfy his craving for love...

Jennifer sighed as the sensuous warmth in her belly moved up to her breasts, exploring their relaxed shape, insinuating into the soft cleft between the pillowed mounds and encircling them with—

Jennifer's eyes popped open and crossed to find Rafe nose to nose with her on the pillow.

'Good morning, darling,' he purred, and kissed her as if he had every right to, taking his time, enjoying the muffled sounds she was making as she struggled to separate fact from fantasy.

'What were you dreaming about? You looked like the cat that got the cream,' he murmured, slowly withdrawing with a series of little pecks around her sleepy mouth.

She could feel her temperature go up, and the giveaway flutter of her lashes made him offer her a sultry, knowing grin. 'You were squirming and rolling your hips, and making those sighing little moans you make when you have a man between your thighs...'

She flushed at the wanton image of herself. 'You were touching me!' she accused, looking down at his hands, which were still cupping her breasts. She noticed the faint red marks marring the creamy roundness, patches of whisker-burn and little pink crescents where Rafe's mouth had feasted greedily on her succulent flesh.

'I couldn't resist,' he said, snuggling closer, his lower legs entangling with hers under the bedclothes, which she discovered had been pushed down around their hips. 'You're so sexy when you're asleep, all soft and pliant and innocently arousing. Are you going to breastfeed?'

'Wh-what?'

Her sleep-deprived brain found it difficult to cope with the sudden switch from sexual banter to questions of maternity. Rafe had kept his promise with spectacular success, and mellow, sweet and strong had taken them far through the night. Long after the mountain outside the window had died back into a quiet smoulder, the molten passion had continued to seethe and pulse in the confines of the wide feather bed. Somewhere, also in the dark reaches of the night, they had talked about what Sebastian had done, comparing their versions of the truth, tacitly avoiding any mention of the future. Now he was back to the future with a vengeance.

'The baby? Are you going to suckle our baby at your breasts?' His hands contracted, her soft nipples slipping between his fingers. 'A mother's milk is important for a newborn baby's immunity; it's full of antibodies and guards against all sorts of infections later, even some chronic diseases. If you want to give your baby the best protection, you should breastfeed for at least six months, even a year or more...'

He was looking at her breasts as if they were miracles

of wonder, and she could feel them begin to firm under
his possessive gaze. 'How do you know?' she asked
hoarsely, stunned by his command of the facts.

'I bought a book. I read it coming over here on the
plane.' He lifted his eyes to hers, his expression faintly
defiant. 'That's how I know you can't feel the baby
move inside you yet; it's still only about ten centimetres
long.'

He had been reading up about pregnancy and childbirth? Warning bells began to clang in Jennifer's mind
as his attention returned to her breasts and a faint frown
marred his tanned forehead. He traced around her dark
areola.

'Your nipples are already quite large, and they're going to grow bigger as you become more heavily pregnant...you don't think they might get to be too much of
a mouthful for a tiny baby?'

Jennifer forgot the bells. Ever conscious of her robust
figure, she was prepared to hit back at him until, incredulously, she realised that he was genuinely anxious. Mr
'I bought a book' had gaps in his learning!

'Of course not.' Her tremulous reply was torn between
laughter and anger. 'God doesn't make those kind of
design faults. Breasts are expressly *designed* to feed
babies, whatever their respective sizes.'

He heard the hint of hurt in her tone and shrewdly
guessed its source, the planes of his face tautening. 'And
to give pleasure,' he added huskily, his thumbs pressing
lightly over the stiffening tips. 'I love your womanly
proportions. I love the roundness of your bottom and the
size of your breasts. And I especially like the way your
nipples fill my mouth when I suck them. Last night you
loved me doing that...'

His sexual frankness had its usual devastating effect.
'L-last night was last night,' she said shakily, remem-

bering the caveat she had issued before their lovemaking.

He was remembering it, too, and his rebellious reaction. His thumbs continued to brush back and forth as he watched the lambent glow in her brown eyes grow. His thighs moved against her and she felt the brush of his heavy loins. 'I'd like to watch you feeding our baby.'

She wished he would stop calling it *our* baby. 'Well, you can't, you won't be here. You'll be back in England when the baby's born…'

'I could visit you.' His potent arousal was growing against her belly.

The suggestion crept like a thief into her soul, rifling her treasury of dreams.

'C-come all this way just t-to watch me feed the baby?' Jennifer stammered, watching him edge closer and closer, knowing that she was playing with fire, but unable to resist the lure of the heat.

'That and…other things.' He bent his head and showed her what those other things were, and in a slow, tender, lazy coupling, vastly different from the sizzling passion of the night before, Jennifer learned a new appreciation of her lover's sensuous skills.

Later, lying weak and dewy in the aftermath of his magnificent possession, Jennifer suddenly noticed the angle of the sun in the sky.

She sat bolt upright, dragging the duvet with her.

'What time is it?'

Rafe yawned, scrubbing his fingers through his streaky gold hair. 'I don't know; I took off my watch last night.'

Jennifer had left hers in the bathroom. She hitched up the duvet and lunged across his supine chest to squint short-sightedly at the small digital clock on the bedside table. She let out a little squawk when the blurry numbers swam into focus.

'Oh, no, it's after eleven o'clock!' she discovered, sinking back onto her knees. 'What about the breakfasts? What will everyone be thinking?'

'Maybe they'll think you stayed up late watching Ruapehu erupt and then slept in because you were tired,' suggested Rafe, with a rakishly innocent air.

She hugged the duvet to her breasts, her brown eyes stormy at his teasing.

'Or they could think that you spent all night making mad, passionate love with your husband and then lingered in bed for his morning wake-up call. Everyone knows that most men are inclined to be amorous in the mornings, especially ones who've just come back from a sex-starved excursion to the Amazonian jungle.'

Jennifer's glare became a dignified scowl. She shook her hair behind her shoulders and looked down her sharp nose at him. The disdainful effect was rather ruined by the ruffled nipple peeping at him from the crook of her arm, but he was enjoying the view too much to point it out.

'I know I often wake up with an erection,' he confided cheerfully, for the pure, wicked pleasure of seeing her blush.

She did, her haughty pose completely disintegrating as he continued silkily, 'Of course, having a voluptuous nude threshing about next to me in the throes of an erotic dream probably had something to do with this morning's delectable awakening.'

Pink and flustered, Jennifer massed the duvet around her, preparatory for a dive towards the puddle of pink towelling on the floor, knowing that Rafe was probably going to hang onto his share of the bedclothes so that she would be forced to abandon her cover just short of her goal.

In the event she was wrong; Rafe let go of the duvet as she made her half-spring, half-tumble, and she was able to hurriedly struggle into her bathrobe under the modest shroud, only to emerge and find him lying bold, bare and beautiful on the rumpled white sheet in a disconcertingly similar manner to the love-supplicant in her dreams. Even the slightly out of focus softness around the edges of her vision were vaguely dream-like.

Averting her eyes, she threw the duvet over him and hurried to snatch up the scraps of green silk and lace from the floor.

'I'm going to have a shower—'

'Is that an invitation?' He was rearranging the bedclothes over himself, obviously in no hurry to abandon his—*her*—sybarite bed.

'No!' She made an effort to calm down, nibbling her lip and discovering it felt uncomfortably tender. 'Last night—well, it happened, and I accept my share of responsibility for it, but it's not going to happen a second time...'

'Just a one-night stand,' he agreed blandly, turning the top sheet down over his chest and folding his hands on it in an attitude of deceptive piety.

She felt terrible. She was reducing the most enravishing experience of her life to the status of a fleeting encounter. And she had told him that she hadn't wanted to be involved in any sordid liaisons!

'Tonight things are going to be different,' she announced, tacitly acknowledging that he wasn't simply going to fade out of her life, that the ties between them had become too complex to sever quickly or easily.

He looked at her stubborn face and smoothly pre-empted her argument. 'Of course they will be. Now that we've made love every which way, and got the uncomfortable lust for each other thoroughly out of our systems, we can relax into physical indifference.'

Since he had taken the words right out of her mouth, Jennifer had no right to feel so disappointed. She hid her chagrin behind a tight smile. He made it sound so…so boringly *commonplace*. Perhaps it was—for *him*. Surely nobody got that mind-blowingly good at making love without a lot of practice.

'I'm not in the habit of having one-night stands,' she pointed out.

'Neither am I, although I must admit to a few in my testosterone-driven modelling years. Now I prefer more satisfying relationships. And I'm very careful of my health, so you needn't worry on that score.'

She was embarrassed to realise that it hadn't even entered her head. Her pregnancy had seemed to make a condom superfluous, and with a shock she realised that she had also subconsciously harboured a bone-deep trust in Rafe's regard for her physical well-being.

'If I hadn't already guessed that you hadn't had a great deal of sexual experience, I would have known it as soon as I entered you,' he continued. 'You were very tight. You weren't a virgin by any chance?'

She would never get used to his blunt way of approaching delicate topics.

'No, of course not!' she said, rattled that he should have thought so. Had she been clumsy, inept? 'I think even Sebastian might have drawn the line at arranging a virgin birth!'

'Then it must have been a while for you—I remember you saying you had no prospect of getting pregnant naturally…'

He was obviously angling to know, so she certainly wasn't going to tell him.

'And for you, judging from your hurry to get me into bed,' she snipped.

'My last long-term companion dumped me ten months ago when she decided that I meant what I'd said all along about not ever marrying her.'

Jennifer's eyes widened. 'You haven't had sex in ten months?'

'I've been busy.' He grinned at her expression, teasing, 'I know you think of me as your rampant sex-god, but I do perform other functions in life. Just because I'm good at it doesn't mean I'm profligate with my talent. If anything it's the reverse—once you've experienced how intense sex can be with the right person, you get bored with bonking the fluff.'

'You weren't bored last night,' she accused hotly, incensed at being reduced to a casual 'bonk'. That was even less meaningful than a one-night stand!

His grin widened. 'But you're not a piece of fluff, darling, you're my wife.'

She slammed the bathroom door on his smirking face and then had to go back out and fetch her clothes, attempting to ignore the way he rolled over to watch her, his green eyes following her from wardrobe to drawer, to dressing table and back to the bathroom.

'Don't use all the hot water, honey,' he sang out after her in a parody of domestic affection.

If it wasn't for the need to save water she *would* have run the *en suite* bathroom's small hot water cylinder cold, but she had to settle instead for rifling the toiletries he had placed on the shelf next to her things and maliciously running the battery of his expensive electric razor flat by shaving her legs with it and then leaving it to buzz on a towel while she had her quick shower.

Having washed and blowdried her hair the previous night, she was forced to linger over cleaning her teeth until the razor gave its last, sick cough and puttered into silence. Now he would have to recharge it before he gave that designer stubble a graze, and her petty sense of revenge had her smiling as she returned to the bedroom warmly dressed in a green tartan skirt and pale yellow blouse.

Rafe had gone out onto the balcony, and she was relieved to see that he had donned his drawstring pyjama trousers.

'Looks like the mountain has gone back to belching just steam and ash,' he said, coming back inside and shutting the doors against the strongly sulphurous smell, the skin on his torso puckered from the southerly chill. 'The wind seems to be pushing the plumes higher, but it's difficult to tell because the sky is pretty grey and there's still a low haze drifting this way.'

His bare feet made slight tracks on the floor, and Jennifer remembered that after their sizzling little piece of foreplay on the balcony the glass doors had stood open for some time before Rafe had got up and closed them during the night. Fine ash had sifted over the polished floorboards by the doors and she hoped that it hadn't drifted as far as her desk. Her computer, inclined to be a little bit temperamental, would not take kindly to volcanic dust clogging its cyberpores.

A loud thump against the door to the stairs made Rafe glance at her with a droll expression.

'Someone come to complain about their breakfast, do you think?'

Another thud made the door shake, and she hurried across the room.

'It's just Bonzer, head-butting the door,' she explained. 'He usually comes up in the mornings.'

But when she opened the door it wasn't only Bonzer, but Milo, too. The cat strolled under the dog as he bounced forward and his paw accidentally clipped her ear. With an offended yowl Milo took off, springing onto the bed, and, ecstatically responding to the unexpected game, Bonzer followed.

'No, Bonzer, no!' cried Jennifer ineffectually as cat and dog careered around the room, barking and yowling.

'Catch him!' she yelled to Rafe as Bonzer shot past

him for the third time, but he was laughing too much, for it was obvious the nimble cat was taunting her clumsy pursuer by sticking to the high points of furniture while the dog dashed a parallel course at floor level.

Finally Milo made a mistake, leaping onto the top of the woven laundry basket, which looked stable enough for a doggy brain to figure it would support a more substantial weight.

Cat, dog and laundry basket went flying, and the last Jennifer saw of the two guilty animals they were racing down the stairs, Bonzer trailing a shocking-pink lace demi-bra from the buckle on his collar and with a transparent stocking flying like a flag on his tail.

'Anyone who sees him is going to think he's a decadent dog who's come off a hard night on the tiles,' chuckled Rafe as he crouched to pick up the overturned basket. 'Hello...what's this? Do you usually wash books along with your sexy under—'

He stopped, rocking on his haunches as he picked up one of the slim paperbacks and recognised the familiar black-edged cover.

'Well, well, well...' His stunned eyes rose speculatively to her appalled face. 'I see you're a fan of Velvet Books...apparently a *big* fan,' he added, stirring the betraying pile.

'I—I—'

'Why keep them in with your dirty laundry? Is that supposed to be an ironic commentary on their contents?'

Thank God he didn't realise that the books *were* her dirty laundry!

'Or were they hidden away for my benefit?' he guessed shrewdly. 'I noticed a few gaps on your bookcase. You don't have to be ashamed that you enjoy erotic stories, Jennifer...nobody should have to apologise for their leisure reading. And I can attest to the fact that Velvet Books are well crafted and well written, and

they're specifically written *by* women *for* women. I'm
the one who developed the line from a small, under-
staffed, under-invested part of the company into a major
publishing success.'

'I— I'm not ashamed,' she lied.

'Then why care whether I see them or not?' he said.
He began to stack the slender books in a pile, noting the
titles. 'I see Lacey Graham is your favourite. I guess
you've realised from the setting of her books that she's
a New Zealander? We have two Kiwis writing for us
and five Australians—about two hundred and forty regular writers worldwide, and more unsolicited manuscripts
than we can handle since we moved up-market and began establishing a mainstream readership. Lacey's one
of our hottest sellers, and I'm grooming her to be number one...'

'*You're* grooming her?' Jennifer grabbed the oak slats
of the curving bed-end, her legs feeling like wet noodles
as she watched Rafe carry the books over to the bookcase and begin plugging the gaps.

'I've been her editor ever since I took over Velvet
Books and started revitalising the line.'

'*Sariel?*' All oxygen had vanished from the room,
leaving her lungs only a breathy wheeze.

He looked up sharply. 'What did you say?'

'I said, seriously? Are you really?' Jennifer impro-
vised shrilly, slurring the words.

There was only one way she could possibly know that
the name of Lacey Graham's editor was Sariel.

He tapped one of the books against his chin, studying
her wilting figure thoughtfully. She hated that look; it
seemed to reach deep down inside her and plunder her
mysteries.

'What's she like?' she asked, hoping to throw him off
the track. 'Is she attractive?'

'Her mind certainly is; I don't know about the rest of

her.' He slotted the book into place and watched her nervous smile flutter as she tried to act like an eager fan.

'Why not?'

'Because we've never met. All our dealings with each other are by letter, via a firm of lawyers in Auckland.'

Her legs began to regain some of their strength. 'What about her voice? Haven't you ever spoken to her on the telephone?'

'She prefers the written word. She lives somewhere fairly isolated and says she resents the encroachment of modern technology on her privacy. If I ever need to communicate with her urgently I send a fax or an E-mail to the lawyer.'

Who then promptly faxed or E-mailed it on to Jennifer!

She had never meant her writing to be taken seriously. It had just been a secret pleasure, a stimulating hobby with which to relieve the boredom and tension of everyday life when she had been struggling to support her slowly convalescing mother. Abandoned by her fiancé, missing dreadfully the brother to whom she had been so close and coping with several emotionally demanding jobs, as well as constantly presenting a cheerful front to Paula's frightening fits of depression, Jennifer had desperately needed a harmless way to let off steam.

Her mother had probably believed her young daughter was going to the altar as a virgin, but Jennifer and Michael had been unable to restrain their ardour, and after their engagement had been broken Jennifer had found herself missing those private lovemaking sessions at his flat, where she had been able to give her passionate nature free rein, secure in the knowledge of their loving relationship. She had been shocked when her physical desires didn't fade away after she relinquished her love. Not wanting to risk going through the same agony of rejection with another man, she had thrown herself into

creating safe fantasies about wildly passionate heroines
and impossibly sexy heroes who *never* rejected each
other.

Writing erotic stories had proved enormous fun. The
secret vice had made her feel dangerously naughty while
at the same time allowing her to remain totally in control
of the events she was describing. The adrenaline rush of
writing them also conveniently sublimated her sex drive.
As her inhibitions over seeing her words in print loos-
ened, her brief sexual fantasies grew longer and more
involved, the writing more explicitly erotic, her charac-
ters more complex and plots more complicated until
she'd realised that she had the equivalent of two short
novels stored on her computer.

She would never have plucked up the courage to do
anything with them if, one day, the wind hadn't whisked
away one of the discards she was burning in the garden
incinerator and been fielded by Sebastian. He had teased
her that the scorching words hardly needed a match to
ignite them, but instead of betraying her secret or scoff-
ing at her efforts he had told her he could recommend
her to a contact at a London publishing house which
specialised in women's erotica.

Jennifer had been far too timid to take him up on it,
but Sebastian, after he had got back to London, had sent
her the publishing house's address and told her that she
could deal in complete anonymity if she chose—even
the publisher need not know her real name if she cared
to go to the bother of concealing it through an agent or
lawyer—and that a number of Velvet authors chose to
similarly protect their identities for both personal and
professional reasons.

Four years later Jennifer had nine books to the credit
of 'Lacey Graham' and two more in the works, and still
hadn't figured out a way to admit to her mother that the
majority of her income was now coming from something

other than the bed and breakfast business. The last six-monthly payment of royalties had been the most substantial yet, and her editor had been encouraging her to be even more prolific.

Her editor.

Her interest had been piqued three years ago, when her previous, female editor had left Velvet and a witty letter had arrived from the new one, jokingly introducing himself under the pen-name 'Sariel', a play on Jennifer's persistent refusal to provide any personal information about herself. She had replied in similar vein, saying that a fantasy editor was the perfect choice for a fantasy writer, and that she appreciated the added buffer from reality since she found the idea of working with a male rather inhibiting. That exchange had set the tone for their diverting professional relationship. Lacey had remained Lacey and Sariel had remained Sariel ever since. The fact that he was male had been less important than the fact that he proved a superbly inspirational editor and an extremely entertaining correspondent.

She realised that Rafe was wearing 'that look' again, and hastily said, 'Well, I guess she has good reason for avoiding interruptions. Most writers are rather solitary by nature, aren't they?'

'Mmm? Oh, yes, I suppose so.' Instead of placing the last book on the shelf with the others he began to idly thumb through it. From the title she realised it was one of her earlier works, written before he had become her editor.

'Do you, uh, work with many other writers?' She wanted to know whether her 'special' relationship with Sariel was so special after all.

'Not directly. I selected a few I thought had special potential to work with when I first took over as editorial director, but I'm mainly in a consulting role now that Velvet is strongly established. I kept Lacey, though, because we're such a successful combination it would be a shame to break us up, and working with her still gives me an enormous kick...' He smiled down at the page, whether at something he read or at his own thoughts she couldn't tell.

So now she was a kept woman. Kept by Raphael Jordan. Father of her child. Goodness, he was already paying her child support and he didn't even know it!

Far from being a stranger, in some ways Rafe knew her almost as well as she knew herself. No wonder they had been so attuned to each other in bed—they had been sharing erotic fantasies for years!

Although she knew he must be very familiar with her work, and was probably regarding it with a serious professional eye, it gave her a shivery feeling of vulnerability to see him leafing through her book.

'Here, I'll put that back if you want to go and have your shower,' she offered, attempting to slip it out of his hand.

He waited until her fingers were almost touching it, then snapped it closed and tucked it under his arm. 'No, thanks,' he said. 'I think I'll re-read it. I did read Lacey's backlist when I took over as her editor, but I only vaguely remember what this one was about.'

He watched her seethe in thinly veiled frustration, intrigued by the definite tinge of urgency in her haste to get him off the subject of Lacey Graham. She was embarrassed, certainly, but there was something more...

'I'm sure there are other books here that you *haven't* read that you'd find interesting,' she was lecturing him. 'Ones that were written for *men*...'

He bit back a smile at the unspoken 'real' hanging in the air before 'men'. She *must* be desperate if she was standing there, pregnant with his baby, her body barely cooled from their hot night of love, trying to hint that he was less than masculine.

'I'm sure there are, but I'm not sexist in my reading habits. I want to read this one.' He patted the book under his arm. 'In fact, while I'm here I might re-read the whole set of Lacey Grahams.' He paused. 'Does that bother you, Jennifer?'

She bared her teeth at him. 'Of course not. But doesn't that make it a bit of a busman's holiday?'

'Not if I read them for *pleasure*,' he told her, effectively securing the last word as he sauntered off to the bathroom, still carrying the book.

Jennifer stumped downstairs to track down her dog-napped underwear, then had to hear her mother's fond assurances that naturally they hadn't expected the honeymoon couple to join them for breakfast.

'We're not on our honeymoon, Mum,' she protested, firmly shutting the door on memories of last night.

'No, but you can pretend,' said Paula, using her stick to limp back and forth across the living room floor as she sorted out cartons of clothes and magazines for the church bazaar. 'Anyway, the Wrights didn't get up for breakfast, either. They said they didn't get in until gone three a.m., but they got some marvellous footage of the eruption. I gave them some muffins and pikelets and a flask of coffee in lieu of breakfast, and they went off to see if the Department of Conservation would let them film some of the lahar sites. Do you think you'll ever wear this again, Jen?'

Her mother held up a crocheted orange mini-dress and Jennifer couldn't help smiling. She had been a schoolgirl when she last wore it. Her mother was a sentimental pack-rat. When Jennifer had converted the attic to a bedroom Paula had insisted on moving everything to the garage, and only when they had been unable to get the car in far enough to shut the door had she consented to winnowing out the chaff.

'I don't think so. Certainly not in the next six months,' she said drily.

'Did you get a chance to tell Rafe about the baby?'

Jennifer busied herself with sorting and folding. 'Yes.'

'I'd bet he was surprised.'

'You'd lose; he'd guessed already.' She felt mean when her mother's face fell.

'Oh.' She rallied. Once having conquered her depression, Paula had been resolute in finding silver linings. 'But I'll bet he was pleased.'

'He was...' She looked at her parent's brightly expectant blue eyes and sighed. 'He was pleased. It's just—being an only child and not having a very good relationship with his own father, I suppose he's a bit wary of what it entails.'

'Well, he strikes me as being a very determined man,' said Paula. 'I think that if he wants something badly enough he'll succeed in achieving it through sheer force of will if necessary.'

Jennifer had ample evidence of that. He had badly wanted her last night and he had certainly achieved *that* goal, though not, she admitted, purely from force of will. He had succeeded because, in spite of her insistence to herself that she was only interested in sex, Rafe already had a piece of her heart. Attracted as she had always been to him physically, it was the deeply sensitive man that she had glimpsed beneath the mocking cynic who had truly exerted the most powerful appeal. As soon as she had learned that he was the father of her baby she had felt a shocking sense of recognition, of inevitability, of jealousy and possessiveness that had sent her shooting off in the opposite direction. But she hadn't been able to outrun either Rafe or her own confused feelings. And now that she knew he was also Sariel he had unknowingly established another claim on her emotions—he was someone she liked and respected, and as Lacey Graham she knew her respect was reciprocated.

Respect and liking, however, were the last things she felt when Rafe came downstairs in jeans, white shirt and a shearling-lined corduroy jacket to receive her mother's lavish congratulations on his impending fatherhood. For he was still carrying her book, tucked visibly in the side pocket of his jacket.

He acknowledged her furtive glare with a grin as he told her mother that, no, he didn't care if it was a son or daughter, as long it was healthy and had Jennifer's beautifully expressive brown eyes.

Then he charmingly offered to help with their task.

'Oh, you don't have to do that, Rafe. You sit down and relax. You're on holiday. You deserve some rest after your marathon experience in the jungle. Dot says it's very physically draining, working in that type of climate.'

'I do feel rather physically drained after my recent experiences,' said Rafe, his mocking glance at Jennifer leaving her in no doubt as to the exact experiences he had in mind. 'But once you acclimatise yourself to a place or activity it's amazing how quickly you re-energise and find yourself ready for action again. Really, I'd like to help.'

'Well, you can do the magazines, then, since you're in the publishing business. Jen, you help Rafe—I'll do the clothes.'

'These are all at least ten years old!' discovered Rafe as he dug down to the bottom of the box.

'The box has been in the garage for years. Mum probably picked them up second-hand herself,' said Jennifer, with a sudden qualm. 'Some of these things are endlessly recycled around the various charity bazaars. Let's just put them all in—'

'Hey, I was featured in some of these.' Rafe's unshaven face was boyishly eager as he unearthed a few dusty copies of English *Vogue* and riffled through the pages. He looked ludicrously disappointed when he failed to find what he was looking for, and frowned as he ran his finger up the centre fold.

'The pages've been cut out!' He sounded as outraged as if someone had removed the frescoes from the Sistine chapel, and with an inner smile Jennifer realised that he had wanted to show off, to display his pride like a peacock to her admiring gaze.

'We probably used them to line Fergus's cage,' she couldn't resist saying, knowing she was making a noose for her own neck.

Sure enough, her mother punished her for her mean-spiritedness. 'More likely they're in Jen's scrapbook. Maybe you didn't know, but Sebastian used to carry a picture of you from *Esquire* magazine folded up in his wallet.'

Colour ran up under the tanned skin of Rafe's face and he looked down at his hands. 'No, I didn't know. He was always insulting about my choice of career.'

'Well, he showed it to us the first time we met him,' Paula continued gently, 'and told us that you took after your mother in looks and him in brains. After that, whenever Jen saw a picture of you in any of the old magazines I bought, she'd cut it out and put it in a book to show Sebastian the next time he came.'

Rafe's flush didn't fade as he turned to look at Jennifer, an arrested expression in his eyes. 'You mean I was your pin-up years before you even met me?' he murmured, the corner of his mouth turning up.

More than he knew!

'I didn't pin you up, I taped you down,' she said tartly.

'Sounds kinky, darling. Did I like it?'

'I was young and impressionable,' she said primly. 'You were the only famous, glamorous person I knew.'

'But you didn't know me.'

'By proxy I did.'

'Our relationship obviously started the way it was intended to go on,' he said drily, and then had to reintroduce the ubiquitous Amazon when Paula wanted to know what he had meant.

Dot came in from dusting her garden and they had a casual lunch of thick vegetable soup and home-baked bread rolls. While they were eating Rafe suggested that an ideal marketing ploy for Beech House might be to take advantage of Paula's special talents and offer residential cooking classes that would enable them to charge a premium rate for the combined accommodation and lessons. That led to a discussion of other, more fanciful ideas, but when Rafe talked about the potential of the upstairs bedroom being a luxury suite for those guests who didn't like sharing a bathroom, Jennifer felt constrained to point out that it was already occupied.

'True, but what if you didn't live here any more?'

Her eyes flashed a warning at him. What on earth was he trying to do?

'All of this is speculation, anyway. Mum couldn't possibly cope—' she began sharply.

'Well, now, dear, that's not quite true,' Paula interrupted mildly. 'I coped while you were away, and Susie has indicated she could work quite a few more hours. And there's Dot, of course. And if we needed any handiwork doing there's always Fergus—and he could help with the business end as well!'

Jennifer stared at her mother in consternation. Was she going mad?

'I don't see how a one-legged budgie is going to be much help when the roof needs patching, and I doubt that he can count to one, let alone do double-entry bookkeeping!'

She heard Rafe shout with laughter as her mother said,

'Not Fergus the bird. Fergus McDonald, from the Gourmet Club. I'm sure you met him, Jen, at one of the church dinners. He's a retired builder and he says he's always looking for something useful to do.'

'And someone to do it with,' added Dot darkly.

Jennifer watched as her mother turned pink and patted her hair.

Her mother? And a *man*?

She turned her accusing gaze on Rafe. This was all his fault. He was the one turning her life inside out and upside down, and now he was dragging her family into the conspiracy!

CHAPTER EIGHT

HE KNEW.

He knew.

All day, Jennifer couldn't shake off the uneasy feeling that Rafe knew more than he was letting on. It wasn't anything he said, it was rather what he did. He trailed her everywhere, helping her make the beds and change the towels, do what laundry could go in the drier, because she didn't want to risk hanging anything out in the still hazy air, relighting the fire and washing the windows with carefully measured amounts of water.

He insisted on sweeping the ash off the verandahs and rinsing down the paths and parking area himself, with buckets of water from the garden pond, because he didn't think a pregnant woman should breathe in too much dust—'It would be as bad as smoking'—and when she wrapped up warmly and took Bonzer for a walk in the gardens, and to fetch the mail from the end of the drive, he accompanied her, asking innumerable questions about Paula and her father and, when she mentioned him, her brother Ian, managing to ferret out of her the reasons for her broken engagement.

'So your first love turned out to have feet of clay.' He dismissed Michael with a contemptuous shrug. 'If he wasn't prepared to stick around when the going got tough, what kind of husband would he have made?' he growled. 'If I was in love with a woman and we had a problem, we'd work it out together.'

Jennifer felt a frisson of hope at his words. But then she reminded herself that any woman who could make a cynic like Raphael Jordan fall in love with her would

137

have to be very special—and very brave! 'I didn't think you believed in love and commitment, or making promises.'

'It's not love and commitment I have the hang-up about, it's marriage. Watching my father ring the changes was a great incentive to bachelorhood. And I have no problem making promises; I simply refuse to make any that I know I won't keep.'

'What about your mother, hasn't she married again?'

'Twice, not happily. I think she was looking for another Sebastian. He was the one she really loved, but she had too much pride and self-respect to live with a man she couldn't trust, and he couldn't forgive *her* for not forgiving *him*.'

Of the three of them perhaps it was the child, Raphael, who had ultimately been the most damaged by the break-up, she thought as they walked the lolloping dog back to the house, her heart aching at this new insight into his character. No wonder he was so determined not to marry; to Raphael, family life was synonymous with uncertainty and turmoil rather than security and happiness. But now that he was faced with the reality, not just the abstract of fatherhood, he was being forced to confront issues which had shaped his adult values, perhaps realising that he had deep-seated needs that his prejudices had hitherto refused to acknowledge.

Her tender feelings didn't stop her feeling exasperated when Rafe continued his campaign of friendly helpfulness, especially when the helping always managed to involve some kind of touching. Finally, when she was setting up the ironing board in her usual spot by the fire in order to do her most disliked chore in comfort, she got fed up with his hovering and snapped at him that it was a one-woman job.

'In that case I'll just quietly read my book while I

keep you company,' he said, taking the wind out of her sails.

Which he did. He sprawled full-length on his back on the couch and read his Lacey Graham, the shush of the turning pages competing with the angry hiss of the steam iron and the crackle of the fire. Every now and then, when Jennifer looked at him out of the corner of her eye, she would find pensive green eyes staring at her over the top of the open book, then the thick lashes would fall and she would see the rapid flickering movements under his lids as he read on down the page.

Jennifer could feel the pressure inexorably building in her skull, like lava pushing up a blocked vent.

'Do you have to stare at me like that?' she erupted at last, after scorching one of their best table napkins trying to second-guess his thoughts.

'Sorry, was I staring?' His reflective gaze sharpened as she flicked her hair behind her ear and nervously adjusted her spectacles. 'I was just wondering...'

'Well, wonder in another direction,' she said, picking up another napkin.

'Listen to this.' He put a finger to the page. '"The man in the shadows stepped into the light—"'

'Those books aren't written to be read out loud,' she interrupted hastily, certain he was going to taunt her with her boldly explicit prose.

'But listen.'

She was disconcerted when he read out a passage which was a physical description of the book's hero, a lustful billionaire, who had kidnapped the prim, unawakened heroine and whisked her to his private tropical island to ravish and seduce her into being his sex slave, only to find the tables turned when his innocent captive discovered the true sensuality of her own nature. She even tied him to the bed at one stage, Jennifer remembered.

'Well?'

She hastily wiped off her dreamy smile. 'Well, what?'

'Don't you think he sounds familiar?'

'I've read the book, so of course it sounds familiar,' she said stiffly, saying a rude word under her breath as she saw the brown mark on the crocheted edging of the napkin.

'No, I mean, don't you think the character sounds like me?'

Her scalp prickled. 'No!'

'*Very* like me.' He looked down at the page and picked out the salient points again—eyes, hair, face shape, height, build, lean athleticism... 'You'd almost think she was describing a picture of me,' he mused.

A picture of him lounging against a white pillar staring sullenly at the camera and wearing nothing but a famous brand of jeans and a sneer. At least she had had the sense to make her heroine a flaming redhead!

'Don't flatter yourself. It's an idealised generic *type*, that's all. You can't take a word-picture as literally as you can a visual representation,' she said, driving the iron across the third white linen square.

'Come to think of it, Lacey's most successful heroes have always been light-eyed blondes,' he commented.

'There's no accounting for taste,' said Jennifer, concentrating intently on her difficult task.

'Mmm.' In the periphery of her vision she could see him tuck one hand behind his head, fanning open his jacket, as he lowered the open book to rest page-down against his white shirt. 'It must be your taste too, or you wouldn't be such a fan of her books,' he pointed out.

Jennifer's eyes narrowed on the knife-edged crease she was making along the folded edge of a napkin.

'And you did say that you asked for blond sperm.'

Jennifer slammed the iron down flat. 'Keep your voice down!' she hissed, looking furtively around, even though

she knew Dot had gone for a nap and her mother was
baking. In her feverish imagination even Fergus seemed
to be leaning a little further on his perch, in order to
eavesdrop on their conversation.

'Well, you did,' he answered in a theatrical whisper.
'You asked for your ideal man, didn't you: big, blond,
sexy...'

Never, never in a million years would he get her to
confess to the eye-colour she had ticked on the clinical
form.

'I never asked for sexy!' she spluttered.

'You needed virile, though, which amounts to the
same thing. Maybe you would have got me even if my
father *hadn't* interfered.'

It was a devastatingly seductive thought.

'But, since intelligence was top of my list, that would
certainly have eliminated you,' she said, using acid to
counteract the sweet surge in her breast.

He grinned, supremely secure in his own intellect. 'I
thought you were supposed to be steaming those things,
not smoking them.'

Jennifer groaned as she lifted the iron and saw the
smouldering ruin of the third napkin. At this rate they
were going to have no table linen left.

'You should have asked me for help after all,' he said
smugly propping up the book again. 'I do all my own
ironing at home.'

Jennifer had enough. 'Good, then you can do the rest,'
she said, emerging from behind the ironing board and
snatching the book out of his hand. 'And *I'll* do the
reading.'

She was reluctantly impressed when he meekly took
over the job without turning a hair, but unfortunately,
just as she was about to spirit the book safely back upstairs, she was waylaid by Margaret Carter, who was

taking off her padded jacket to hang on the brass hook beside the door.

'Oh, Jennifer, I hope it's not too late, but we were wondering if you could possibly do dinner for us tonight?' There was an apologetic smile on her plump, seamed face as she took off her headscarf and draped it over her jacket. 'The roads are awfully dusty—after we went through Turangi, every time we passed a car it was like being caught in a sandstorm. I don't think Ron likes the idea of navigating after sunset, and we don't want to get stranded again, as we were yesterday.'

'Of course we can,' smiled Jennifer, clasping the book behind her back in her linked hands. 'Mum is doing her famous pheasant cassoulet, with a feijoa and banana flan for dessert. Did you have a good cruise yesterday?'

'Yes, and they gave us a wonderful lunch. But it was rather cold out on the lake. And when we woke up this morning there was a layer of dirty ash all over the town. Do you think it's going to snow and make things clean again? It's getting rather nippy out there.'

She ventured into the living room, looking for the fire, as her husband came up the front steps, jingling his car keys and looking very spry for a rotund man of middle years. Belatedly Jennifer remembered Rafe, and nervously trailed Ron Carter's heels, but she found herself too late to take control of the introductions.

'You must be the bloke who's been in the Amazon,' said Ron Carter, enthusiastically pumping Rafe's hand when his wife told him that he was Jennifer's husband. 'One day deep in the wilds, the next deep into domestication,' he joked, nodding at the ironing.

Rafe's eyes had gone first to the clerical collar and then to the bluff, open face with its wide smile. 'Each has its own merits,' he admitted, with an answering grin.

'Raphael—were you named for the painter? People often grow up to bear out their names. I remember Paula mentioning you were doing the photography on your expedition,' said Margaret.

'Actually, I was named for one of the seven archangels,' Rafe said modestly. As well he might—he was certainly no angel, thought Jennifer. 'It's a tradition in my mother's family. Her brothers are Gabriel, Raguel and Michael.'

'So that leaves you Uriel, Sariel and Jerahmeel for *your* sons.' The Reverend Carter completed the set with a chuckle and Jennifer's eyes flew to Rafe's face in shocked recognition as he demurred at the idea of saddling children with unusual names.

Of course he noticed her sharply reactive look, and, thinking that it might be wise to escape his perceptive eye Jennifer began edging towards the door, only to collide with Dot and feel the book behind her back slipping out of her hands.

It bounced with a thud off Dot's sturdy brown lace-up, ending cover-up on the floor, the elegant grainy black and white photo of a male torso on the front cover seeming to Jennifer's guilty mind to shriek its contents long and loud to the room. In fact it was only a few seconds before she and Dot simultaneously bent to scoop it up.

Dot's stubby hand got there first. She perused the cover photo, her thick silver eyebrows descending over her black pebble eyes as she flipped it over and read the blurb on the back. 'Haven't read this, have I?'

'I doubt it,' said Jennifer in a strangled voice. 'Uh, I don't think it's your kind of book.'

'I'm old but I ain't *dead*,' Dot told her with a little snort that indicated she recognised exactly what kind of book it was. She handed it back. 'Everybody needs a little spice in their life now and then. I've read some pretty hair-curling things in my time...'

Since her hair was now dead straight, Jennifer guessed

that they had had no permanent effect. Murmuring a reply, she beat a hasty retreat before the Reverend and his wife decided to get in on the literary discussion.

She stowed the book back on her bookshelf and hurried over to her desk, thinking that while Rafe was chained to the ironing board she would do a little catching up on her computer. She carefully wiped down the casing with a damp cloth to ensure it was free of volcanic dust before switching it on, and entered the two bookings she had received in the mail into her files, printing out confirmation letters that she would get Susie to post. Then she brought her expenses up to date and typed out her mother's recipes and notes for the next day's cooking class.

A printer jam had her cursing, and while she was trying to clear it her mother called on the intercom phone and told her that there was a tradesman at the door offering to spray the ash off the roof and out of the gutters and downpipes using his own tanker of water. Jennifer went downstairs and after intense discussion decided she wanted to wait a few days to see what the mountain was going to do before she spent money on a job that might have to be done all over again. Several other minor distractions intervened before she remembered that she had left the computer suspended in mid-task, and by that time Rafe had finished his ironing and had inevitably ended up wherever he could cause her the most trouble.

'What are you doing?' she demanded as she walked in to find him swivelling idly in her chair, snooping through her operating system.

'I fixed your printer problem,' he said, pointing to the neat stack of papers on the desk. 'And you had an awful lot of conflicts in your system so I cleaned up the clutter on your hard disk for you. Don't you run your diagnostic programme regularly?'

'If I don't have a problem I don't see the need to go

hunting for one,' said Jennifer, silently praising her fore-thought in deleting her compromising files.

'Ah, well, there we differ. I like to seek out potential trouble and deal with it *before* it can develop into a serious problem.'

He was talking about more than computers, he was expressing a philosophy of life, and Jennifer wondered if she and her baby were classed as 'potential trouble' or 'a serious problem'. Her heart clenched in her chest as she wondered how he intended to 'deal' with it.

'I see you're on the Internet,' he added as the screen registered his arrival back at the desktop, and she reached over his shoulder and smartly tapped the escape button, shutting down the computer, grateful that her password would have prevented him browsing too close to her secrets.

'You're welcome to plug your laptop into the phone-line if you want to use a computer,' she said pointedly, having noticed the slimline case amongst his bags.

He accepted the metaphorical slap on the wrist with remarkably good grace, swinging around in the chair to face her. 'Thank you, if I'm going to be here a while, that would be useful.'

'A while?' she echoed, putting her hand to her stom-ach.

'An indefinite period,' he clarified with beguiling soft-ness, a disturbing gleam of elation in his eyes as he wooed her with his possessive look. 'A period of dis-covery, adjustment and adaptation...'

A combination of fear and uncontrollable longing scrambled her brains. 'Won't your mini-empire collapse if you're not there to run it? Don't you have important things to do—places to go, people to see?' she said, nervously pushing her glasses up her nose.

'Not at the moment, no. I think I have my priorities straight, and I've always believed in delegation—my

employees are used to acting on their own initiative.' He
got to his feet and looked down into her blustering confusion with a terrifyingly tender smile of understanding.
'Right now *you're* the most important thing in my life.'

He had a masterly gift with an exit line, thought
Jennifer dumbly as she watched him calmly saunter out
through the door. He couldn't possibly understand how
she felt, so how *dare* he make her feel so…so wretchedly wonderful and stupidly cherished.

'Right now' didn't mean tomorrow, she was still reminding herself fiercely as she helped her mother with
the last-minute preparations for dinner. 'Right now' was
a warning, not a promise, telling her that Rafe's interest
in her was only temporary. Once he had solved the
'problem' she represented, he would go back to the sophisticated life in which she could have no part.

And anyway, she wasn't a *thing*, she seethed; she was
a person with her own feelings and thoughts and *plans*.
Plans which she had not permitted to include Raphael
Jordan. Rafe was the stuff of heady fantasy, not of practical reality. It should be enough for her to know that
she would soon have his son or daughter to lavish with
all her love and adoring attention—which would surely
be wasted on the baby's father!

In spite of her worst anxieties, dinner was miraculously easy. Jennifer had difficulty believing that it was
simply out of respect for Ron Carter's clerical collar, but
for whatever reason Rafe subdued his wicked streak of
rebellious mischief and was almost as angelic as his
namesake as he conversed with the vicar and his wife
on the subject of preserving ethnic cultures without once
mentioning the tribes of the Amazon.

When Ron and Margaret mentioned that they lived in
Wellington, Jennifer learned that Rafe had turned
twenty-one there, on his way to a working holiday at the
Coronet Peak ski fields near Queenstown in the South

Island. The skis on his roof rack had obviously not been there just for show, she thought, as he spoke of his hopes that parts of the Whakapapa or Turoa ski fields could be groomed of ash so that he could try out Ruapehu's famous slopes.

Not even when the mention of the mountain prompted Ron to say heartily, 'I understand we missed some thrillingly spectacular goings-on here last night!' did Rafe pick up the gauntlet with one of his fiendish *double entendres*, and it was left to Jennifer to embarrass herself with a nervous burst of giggles.

Dave and Celia arrived back while they all were still having tea and coffee by the fire, and they chatted for a while before the guests began drifting off to their rooms.

Rafe scraped dishes and stacked the dishwasher alongside Jennifer, and Paula leaned on her stick to tell him he was shaping up to be an ideal son-in-law.

'I must get you some brains,' she declared, startling him with one of her frequent *non sequiturs*.

'Uh, what have I done wrong?' He looked down at his stacking to discover his mistake.

'No, I mean to *eat*,' Paula laughed. 'Jenny told me you like that kind of thing.'

'I guess my preferences are changing, then,' he murmured, wiping the smirk off Jennifer's face as he continued, 'Because since I arrived I've developed a taste for something plump and juicy that I can really sink my teeth into…'

The innuendo went entirely over Paula's head. 'I'll do you a nice aged fillet steak for tomorrow night, then.' She beamed.

Plump! Jennifer slammed the dishwasher shut and jabbed the button.

Plump! she smouldered as she and Rafe partnered against her mother and Dot in a game of cards in front of the fire, losing because they kept trumping each other instead of their opponents, then watched a late news report on the television covering the eruption and its aftermath.

Plump! she brooded as she lingered to put the guard in front of the fire and the cover over Fergus's cage before she switched off the downstairs lights and followed Rafe upstairs.

But she was thinking of Rafe's teeth as she ventured reluctantly into her bedroom. His strong, even white teeth, which nibbled and raked and aroused and...oh, hell! yes, all right, she had to admit it...made her feel all plump and juicy inside...

But she had told him that tonight would be different, and for the sake of her sanity as well as her pride she had to stick to her decision. She already knew that Rafe was seriously addictive. One glorious infusion of unbridled delight was all she dared permit herself—two would be getting dangerously close to a habit. Tonight any attempt to taunt or seduce her into forgetting her principles would fall sadly flat!

She had half expected Rafe to have stripped for battle while he was waiting for her, but he was standing beside the bed still fully dressed, although his white shirt was untucked from his jeans and half unbuttoned, and his open cuffs flicked back on his strong wrists.

Jennifer opened her mouth to remind him they would not be sharing a bed, but then he shifted aside and she saw what was on the floor behind him.

She stared at it, a blood-rush of humiliation roaring in her ears. The bedclothes, which had miraculously reappeared in the glory box some time during the morning, were as deftly arranged as they had been the previous night.

'I'll sleep on the floor; you take the bed.'

She stared at his face, as cool as the flatly uninflected

words. Oh, God, had he really *meant* it about having got her out of his system?

'I—you don't have to... I—I'm sure the bed is big enough for both of us to sleep in without encroaching on each other's space,' she stammered, all her intentions of keeping him at a safe distance going up in smoke as she strove to match him for cool indifference.

'I'm sure the bed is, but unfortunately *I'm* not,' he said, his mouth adopting a cynical twist.

'I—I don't understand...' she muttered, caught up in her own agony of embarrassment. Thank God she hadn't blurted out what she had been thinking when she had walked into the room.

'I mean that if *I* don't trust myself, then you certainly shouldn't. If I get into that bed with you, Jennifer, I won't be doing any sleeping. I can't lie within kissing distance of you and think pure thoughts...'

She trembled as his voice roughened, his cool evaporating, his fists clenching at his sides. 'I'd start thinking about what we did last night and I'd get hard. I'd want to touch you, make love to you—do everything that we did together all over again, and more—much, much more...'

Her mouth went dry. 'But this morning you said—'

'I can't believe you were naïve enough to believe me. You're a woman, a sensual, passionate woman, and there was a lot more than sex going on between us last night. That's why you were running scared this morning and trying to set limits on our relationship, to restrict our contact—it was your fight or flight response to danger. And in some ways you're right to worry; I *am* dangerous to you—because I'm not going to meekly accept limits and restrictions,' he said rawly. 'I'm not going to let you push me away because I might disrupt the nice, cosy set-up you have here. I *do* want to disrupt it; I want to disrupt *you*. I need you to look at me and see *me*—not a reflection of your own fears, not Sebastian's son or your baby's father, but *me*, Rafe Jordan the *man*—your lover...'

His unconscious use of the word 'need' rather than 'want' ravished Jennifer's resistance. To be desired was a powerful aphrodisiac, but to be *needed* was infinitely more desirable. It gave her the courage to recognise and accept that her own need to love was greater than her fear of being destroyed by the loving. The blood beat heavily in her veins as she made her decision.

'As long as you realise my baby is more important to me than anything else,' she warned him unevenly, stepping forward as her hands went to the buttons of her yellow blouse. 'Whatever happens between us from now until the time you leave—my baby stays with me...'

His eyes darkened, a corona of flaring gold ringing his expanding pupils within the outer halo of green as he stilled her hands on her buttons. 'Always. I would never, ever separate a loving mother from her child; that's one promise that's easy for me to make.'

The dark intensity of his expression was suddenly slashed by a dazzling smile, a sinful, sexy challenge. 'I hope you're as hungry as I am, darling, because the appetiser is about to be served...'

Holding her gaze, he ripped open the rest of his shirt and threw it on the floor. He unbuckled his belt and unzipped his jeans, again stopping her tentative move to unfasten her blouse.

'No, let me do that.' He stepped back and rapidly stripped off the rest of his clothes. Naked, he slowly unstrapped the watch from his wrist, and dropped it on his clothes. Then, equally slowly, legs astride, he raised his arms and raked his hands through his hair, letting her watch the lift and play of lean, hard muscles, displaying himself unashamedly to her blushing fascination.

'Do you like me?' he asked. As if there was anything

about his magnificent body to *dis*like, she thought dizzily, and nodded.

'You don't mind the scar?' He pointed to an infinitesimal flaw low on the dark golden belly, just above the dense thicket of his groin, his fingers brushing across the bold thrust of his erection as if by accident. But Jennifer knew it wasn't any accident. He had deliberately drawn her gaze to his manhood. He wanted her to look at the swollen shaft, to see how much he wanted her, and to realise that soon she would feel that satiny thickness pushing up into her body again.

'You're the first woman I've ever made love to without using a condom,' he said huskily, frankly enjoying the jolt that went through her at his admission, and the sight of her nipples visibly hardening under the thin material of her blouse. 'That's why I came so fast that first time—it felt so incredibly good to be naked inside you.'

Jennifer could feel her breasts readying themselves for his touch, and a hot moistening between her thighs. In her mind's eye they were already making love, and it was with a shock she felt her hand fisting in her tartan skirt and realised that she was still fully dressed.

She looked up at his face, her eyes glazed, and he tilted his head, saying silkily, 'Does it make you feel powerful and in control, to be wearing clothes while I'm naked?'

No, but it was sinfully erotic.

Before she could answer he had picked her up by the waist and lifted her high against his chest.

'Wrap your legs around my waist,' he ordered gruffly and as she clung to his shoulders and obeyed he carried her across the room to her desk.

Wrapping one arm across her back, he swept the clutter beside the computer to the floor and sat her down on the rounded edge, pushing her thighs apart as he stepped between them, his hands sliding up under her flared skirt, a ripple of hesitation hitting him as he found that she was wearing suspenders and stockings rather than panty-hose. Then his hands were moving up to roughly snatch off her panties, and when she squeaked a protest he covered her mouth with his and stroked her with his tongue.

She fumbled with her glasses as they bumped against his nose, but he wouldn't let her take them off.

'No, leave them on. I want you wearing everything except your panties,' he growled, sending thrills ravishing through her senses.

'Still feel in control?' he murmured mockingly, his fingers touching her intimately, exploring her damp folds. 'Mmm, just how I like you,' he reminded her approvingly, 'sweet and juicy.' And then he was sliding to his knees, replacing his fingers with his mouth, his hair-roughened cheeks grazing the sensitive skin of her inner thighs. Jennifer threw back her head, her spine arching, her hands sinking helplessly into his spiky soft hair.

But no sooner had the pleasure begun to slam into her than he was rising to his feet again, pulling her hips further forward onto the very edge of the desk, ripping open her blouse to expose her transparent bra and tipping her flat on her back as he hooked his arms under her bent knees and mounted her in a single thrust.

As she gasped with shock and moaned with pleasure he dragged away the sheer fabric of her bra with his teeth and began to lick and suck at her jutting nipples in hungry rhythm with the frantic driving of his hips, grunting as her fingers and heels dug into his flexing buttocks, pulling him deeper into her fastness.

It had all happened so quickly that Jennifer had had no time to think, only to feel and react to the erotic stimuli, the familiar words that he was whispering calling forth instinctive replies until their panting cries rose to a simultaneous crescendo and died away in a shuddering of sighs.

After a few moments, without withdrawing from her body, Rafe raised himself on his braced arms and smiled triumphantly down into her drowsy, sated face.

'Well, Lacey, I guess we can both agree *that* chapter works…'

It hit her then—the wicked things he had said to her in the throes of passion, the automatic replies that had floated up from her subconscious—the whole highly charged erotic scenario: starchy secretary and wolfish boss locked in their office suite overnight…a torrid affair conducted on an interesting array of office furniture…

She and Rafe had been re-enacting a scene straight from one of her own books. One, moreover, that hadn't been published yet!

'*Oh!*' She closed her eyes, shutting out his hugely smug face.

'Yes, oh! How much longer did you think you could keep it from me?'

The protective instinct was too strong. 'Keep what?'

Warm lips covering her own made her eyes fly open. She began to struggle and he eased himself from her body and helped her to sit up, but while she tried to straighten her twisted clothes he was busy taking them off.

'What are you doing? Stop that!' she cried, slapping at his hands as he unzipped her skirt.

'I'm levelling the playing field,' he said, plucking off her glasses. 'For the purposes of this discussion there's going to be nothing between us but the raw, naked truth.'

What a terrifying thought! Aftershocks of pleasure were still rippling through her body as she wrestled with him, losing her blouse as well as her skirt to his superior cunning.

'You—you did this to me just to—just to prove some wretched theory!' she choked, hot with humiliation at the idea, hitting out at his hard chest, her fists sliding off his perspiration-slicked skin.

His hand slid around her back to unhook her bra and peel it away from her jouncing breasts. Then he tossed her over his shoulder, ignoring her furious curses and the pounding on his back as he carried her over to the bed and threw her down on the mattress, straddling his body over her squirming bundle of rosy outrage while he unsnapped her lacy garters.

'I did it in the first place because it was an incredibly arousing fantasy and I was curious to know if it would be as hot and wild in real life,' he said, pushing her stockings down her threshing legs. 'It was,' he added roughly, causing her feverish struggles to slacken. 'And secondly, I did it because it was *your* fantasy and *I* wanted to be the man who realised it for you. I'd like to explore all your sexy fantasies with you...'

He lay down beside her, propped up on his elbow, his other arm lying loosely across her waist, and she caught her breath at his sultry expression, letting it out in a huff as he admitted, 'The rest was pure bonus. I was so turned on by the time I got you flat on your back I hardly knew what I was saying—how was I to know you'd confirm your secret identity by sticking so perfectly to your own script?'

The dancing gold glints in his eyes mocked her glowering doubts. She wouldn't put it past him to have ruthlessly planned and executed every single steamy moment of her downfall.

'Come on, darling, 'fess up. It's far too late to pretend you don't know what I'm talking about.'

He wasn't angry at her deception, she realised in sudden wonder, the tight knot of wretched embarrassment loosening its stranglehold on her emotions. If anything he looked soaringly elated, immensely proud of his discovery. Proud of *her*.

'How long have you known? How did you find out?' she mumbled, reaching behind her to pull the duvet over her bare body.

He tugged it to include himself, enfolding them both in a fluffy cocoon of enforced intimacy before slinging his arm back over her waist.

'I'm no mathematician, but I can add two and two,' he told her. 'I had the feeling you were hiding something else from me, but I had no idea what it might be until the books turned up and you *really* began to act guilty— far more so than was warranted by my finding the female equivalent of a stack of *Playboys* stuffed under the mattress. Everything I was learning about you seemed to hint to me in a certain direction, but I couldn't bring myself to really believe it. Not until I happened across your E-mail. You have one, by the way, from a certain firm of lawyers—' His voice turned whimsical '—passing on a message from some guy called Sariel who would like to arrange a meeting with you while he's in New Zealand to discuss a new book contract...'

He had known all evening!

That angelic behaviour at dinner had merely been a calculated attempt to lull her into a false sense of security.

'You *happened* across my E-mail? You logged onto my Internet connection? But you couldn't have!' she protested bitterly, cursing the fact that things had been so hectic in the past few days that she hadn't bothered to check her messages. She *knew* he had been up to no good puttering around her computer. 'I have a secret password!'

He shook his head, baffled at her stupidity. 'Are you kidding? What's secret about it? Don't you know you're *never* supposed to use the names of pets for security passwords? It took me about thirty seconds to find out that it was "Fergus".'

'You shouldn't have been snooping around my computer in the first place!'

He grinned at her rosy-cheeked annoyance. 'I do a lot of things I shouldn't; that's why I'm so successful. Besides, around you, snooping is the only way I get to find out anything interesting. I take it my father was the one who hooked you up with an English publisher?'

She nodded jerkily.

'Lucky for you I rescued it from my blockhead stepbrother, or we wouldn't be celebrating the secret of your success today. He was letting the Velvet line sink into oblivion, but I knew that it had untapped potential.'

His eyes crinkled. 'Rather like our relationship, wouldn't you say?'

Where he saw potential, she saw complications.

'So...what happens now?' she asked warily, wondering what he intended to do with his new knowledge.

He shifted his thigh suggestively over hers.

'Now, my sinful, sexy authoress—we negotiate a new contract!'

CHAPTER NINE

JENNIFER pulled off her helmet and laughed up through her spattered glasses at a saturated Rafe, the adrenaline still pumping through her veins after the swooping ride down the foaming waters of the Tongariro River.

'See, I told you it would be easy!' she teased, flexing arms which ached from paddling under the shouted instructions of the rafting guide. Clad in wetsuits and bulky yellow padded life-jackets, they had got thoroughly wet but not cold, and Jennifer felt as if she was ready to go back up-river and do it all over again. She had rafted down the Tongariro on other occasions, but never had she felt so full of the joy of living.

'I think your "easy" work-out might require a massage with liniment tonight,' he replied wryly, removing his helmet and life-jacket, amused by her bouncing excitement. 'Or if not liniment, something equally stimulating to the circulation. Perhaps...whipped cream?'

The flaring heat in her tawny brown eyes was matched by the sudden glow drying her wet cheeks.

It amazed Rafe that Jennifer still had the capacity to blush and he couldn't resist the urge to constantly test her helpless response to his flirting. He had assumed that a writer of erotic novels would be casually blasé about sex and sexual banter—that was what had thrown him when he had begun suspecting Lacey Graham's real identity—but Jennifer's sizzling fantasy life seemed to make her more, rather than less vulnerable to blushing confusion. She was a strange mixture of sophistication and innocence, boldness and caution, soft feminine yielding and infuriating female stubbornness, and the heady combination had proved deeply alluring to his jaded soul.

'I'm afraid I have other plans for this evening,' Jennifer said, tilting her nose loftily in the air. 'I have a slave-driving editor hounding me to finish my next book.'

'I'm sure he'd want you to get all the proper research done for it first. Perhaps he'd even be willing to offer himself up to the delights of whipped cream—purely in the interests of literary accuracy, of course...'

He walked away, taking with him the immensely satisfying picture of Jennifer drenched in pretty pink.

Jennifer's smile faded as she cleaned her glasses and watched her lover pick his way down the bank to help some of the other raftees lift the big yellow inflatable rafts out of the water and carry them up the steep grade of loose stones, slippery with muddy ash, to where the rafting company's four-wheel drive and trailer were waiting to tow them back for the next group of paying customers.

Her lover.

She still couldn't believe that she, Jennifer Jordan, was having a scorching affair with a man who had threatened to cause her such grief.

Was still threatening to, for that matter.

It was four days now, since he had found out her guilty secret. Four entertaining days and three, long, glorious, passion-filled nights. Long enough for her to realise, to her delight and despair, that he was a man she could love...and *did* love...not wisely but far, far too well.

It wasn't the steady, slowly unfurling emotion she had felt for Michael. This time love was hot and strong and fierce, and it had burst upon her with the impact of a bomb—a time bomb which had lain ticking away inside as she had cut Rafe's photos out of magazines and written him into her fantasies, as she had exchanged friendly and stimulating letters with Sariel, and as she had silently coveted the son of her husband, and secretly yearned for the father of her baby.

It was a love that cared nothing for logic or for reason, and as she watched him walk down the hill Jennifer acknowledged that it was a sight that she would have to get used to: Rafe walking away.

She hadn't asked him how much longer he was staying, for she hadn't wanted to know, and to her relief her mother had not pressed them for their future plans, seeming to assume that husband and wife needed time and privacy to reassimilate their marriage and that they would broach the subject when ready.

Meanwhile Jennifer had given herself permission to suspend her despair and devote herself to basking in the delight. She would sort out the emotional tangle she had created later. In spite of the grief that opening her life to him was storing up, Rafe *was* a delight simply to be with, to talk to, to challenge and even to quarrel with...

He was also good at making sure she didn't take herself too seriously, as she had learned that night in bed, when Rafe had mentioned the negotiation of a contract.

She had bristled with suspicion, demanding to know what contract he was talking about. Looking down into her belligerent face, he had told her it was quite simple: as long as she continued to sleep with him, he would keep all her guilty secrets safe.

'That's blackmail! You're trying to *blackmail* me into having sex with you!' she had screeched at him in a spasm of astonished outrage.

'Yes, and unless you agree to satisfy my evil lusts, you and your mother will be thrown starving into the snow,' he had hissed sibilantly, twirling an imaginary moustache.

'Oh.' She had subsided, mortified by her gullibility,

as she'd recognised his wicked amusement. She would have to learn not to bite at every piece of tantalising bait he dangled in front of her eyes, she'd told herself as his grin widened.

'Wanna try it?' he had drawled provocatively, scraping his whiskers on her naked shoulder. 'Me, the ruthless deflowerer of virgins, and you, the helpless innocent, quivering and begging as I ravish you within an inch of your life?'

'No!'

But he had seen the glint of professional interest in her eye and had fallen back on the bed, shaking with laughter, until she had muffled his mirth by stuffing a pillow into his mouth. Rising to the challenge, he had romped her into giggling submission and made love to her again, in a very simple, straightforward, *very* satisfying way.

So, in the end the only contract there was any negotiation over was the one between their *alter egos*, Lacey Graham and Sariel. Rafe wanted to offer her a greater advance for her next three books, but was suggesting tighter controls on her output, and Jennifer was dubious.

'I've always only written at my own speed; I don't know if I could work to someone else's deadline,' she had said. 'How fast I write depends on what's happening around me, and with the baby coming I need to stay even more flexible.'

She had propped up her elbows on her desk, where they were discussing the draft contract Rafe had produced from his suitcase the morning after they had engaged in a very different form of negotiation on the very same battered surface!

Rafe, having discovered a miracle within his own grasp—his pet protégé, the reclusive authoress he had suspected he would never meet—was determined to make the most of his unexpected opportunity.

'I want to enjoy this baby,' Jennifer told him firmly.
'It'll probably be the only one I have, so I want to spend
as much time as I can being a mother.'

Rafe frowned at the wistful inflection. 'You want
more children?' He sounded faintly hostile, as if he
couldn't understand such a desire.

'I would have liked some more, yes,' she said sharply.
'Michael and I planned to have three.'

The frown turned to a scowl. He tapped his gold pen,
slotted between his finger and thumb, on the notepad in
his lap. 'You're lucky it didn't get that far. He'd probably have ended up walking out on you *and* the kids,
hooking up with someone else who wouldn't make de-
mands on him and skimping on his maintenance.'

His cynicism struck to the heart of her beliefs. 'Just
because children have no place in *your* life doesn't mean
that other men don't care about their offspring.'

'I care,' he rapped. 'I'm here, aren't I?'

Just. It was on the tip on her tongue to say it, but his
pen was tapping at an ominous speed.

'And what about all your other anonymous children?
Do you care about *them*?' she demanded unfairly.

The pen stopped, his knuckles whitening. 'That's different, you damned well know it is! That whole process
is designed to be deliberately detached. I have no in-
volvement or awareness of their conception, therefore no
emotional investment.'

'You had no awareness or emotional investment in
this conception, either.' If only she knew exactly what
was going on inside his head she might be able to put
to rest her secret fears.

The tautening of his expression was an indication that
he realised the futility of the argument. 'But I do have
other, more concrete investments in you, don't I?
Notably the one we're supposed to be discussing. Look,
can we stick to the subject here—?'

'*I* wasn't the one who wandered off it—'

'We were *talking* about your *career*,' he interrupted, his pen beginning to tap again. 'I, of *all* people, should know how much motherhood means to you, but you usually write at night anyway, when the baby will be asleep.'

'Babies don't always keep regular hours, and motherhood is tiring, especially in the early stages. What you're talking about is the equivalent of working almost full-time. I just don't want to over-commit myself.'

'We can be flexible on the deadlines, as long as you give me plenty of notice if you think you're going to run over. Lots of other women authors write while bringing up their families.'

'I'm not other women; I'm me.' Under pressure of his gaze, she snapped, 'Would you mind not doing that with your pen? It's very irritating!'

'Sorry.' He folded his arms and put the pen to his thoughtfully pursed lips, which was even more of a distraction. 'You know, this wouldn't be such a problem for you if you weren't so damned secretive about what you do.'

She was instantly wary. 'I told you last night, Mum would be even more upset about the type of stories I write than she would be about my arrangement with Sebastian.'

'I think you underestimate your mother. Paula's a survivor; she's proved how resilient she can be. I'm sure she'd rise above her embarrassment for your sake. You're good at what you do; that's something for her to be proud of.'

She stiffened at the implied threat. 'If you *tell* her...'

He threw the pen onto the desk, straightening in the hard chair he had brought up from downstairs.

'Damn you, if you can't bring yourself to trust me, at least grant that I'm too good a businessman to risk killing the goose that lays the golden egg! Lacey Graham is a very valuable asset to Velvet. I want to work *with* you, not against you. Stop treating me as if I was the enemy.'

She looked at him incredulously and he ran an impatient hand through his hair. 'You know what I mean...' he muttered, his eyes faintly uncomfortable.

Yes, she did. He meant that although he had swooped down on her home like an avenging archangel, and had angrily blackmailed, lied, harassed and seduced his way into her life, he fully expected her to embrace his bone-deep integrity as a fact of life.

She leaned back in her seat, suddenly enjoying herself. Rafe had dragged her out of bed practically before she was awake to hammer out his offer. She had barely been allowed time to pull on her clothes before he was flourishing his contract under her nose and demanding her full attention to business.

'Maybe I should take advantage of the fact that I'm sleeping with my editor and hold out for a bigger percentage of royalties,' she taunted him.

His eyes narrowed as he ignored the flagrant provocation of the first half of her statement. 'The profit margin per book isn't big enough to offer authors a higher percentage of net. We make our money on volume—our sales grow; your income grows.'

'I suppose another publisher might have something different to say,' she said slyly.

He was too canny to disagree. 'Maybe. But we're the best. If you want to write for the best you write for Velvet Books. And there's another reason it wouldn't be in your interests to write for a rival publisher.'

'Oh, what's that?' she attempted to look bored.

'You own fifteen percent of Velvet Books.'

'I *what*?' She nearly fell off her chair.

It was his turn to sit back and enjoy her consternation.

'You didn't even look at the names on the shares Sebastian left you in his will, or the details of the bequest, did you?' He grinned. 'He left you his minority interest in the company that owns Velvet Books. I own the other eighty-five percent. You and I are business partners.'

Oh, *Sebastian*! Jennifer cringed inwardly. No *wonder* Rafe had been so furious with the disposition of his father's will.

'No, we're not.' She stoutly rejected the tantalising link. 'I told the lawyer I wasn't accepting them.'

'In the event of which, Sebastian provided for a ninemonth holding period for you to change your mind, before they revert to the very person who put them in the toilet in the first place; Lydia's son Frank, remember him? The twerp who asked you if you had silicone implants in your breasts the first time you met.'

The significance of the gestation period of the clause escaped neither of them as he continued wryly, 'Believe me, I'd far rather it was someone with talent and imagination holding the shares than that obnoxious, overeducated cretin, who thinks a soft degree makes him God's gift to business.'

'You *want* me to accept the shares?' she asked, shaken. She had been certain that one of his prime purposes in coming to New Zealand was to ensure the exact opposite.

He shrugged. 'Under the terms of the will you can't sell them for a year after you inherit, and then only to me. There's no restriction on what Frank can do with them, and after my comments on his business acumen he'd never sell to me. So, yes, you and I would both benefit if you kept them.'

'What on earth was Sebastian *thinking*?' Jennifer fretted in exasperation.

Rafe stared at her for a moment from under flat golden

brows. 'Unfortunately he didn't see fit to leave us that information.'

But he could make a very shrewd guess.

Later, Jennifer had had to suffer the embarrassment of asking him to shift the heavy wardrobe so that she could retrieve the files containing her old contracts and letters. Amongst them was a large scrapbook, which she tried to slip casually into a drawer.

Not casually enough. Rafe smiled as he leafed through the newsprint pages, looking at her collection of faded cuttings from glossy magazines, carefully attached with double-sided tape.

'I have quite a few scrapbooks of my own at home,' he conceded off-handedly, consoling her blushes. 'At first it was just for the sake of my portfolio, but later, well…' He gave a rueful shrug. 'I guess I have a healthy streak of narcissism in my soul, and I thought it would be something to show—'

He stopped guiltily and she completed the cliché for him. 'To show your grandchildren?'

He gave her a sidelong glance. 'I *was* going to say, to show people when I'm old and shrivelled,' he lied defensively.

She couldn't imagine such a thing. She was sure that Rafe would mature like a fine wine, growing more impressive with the years. Definitely worth laying down, she thought mischievously.

He stroked a finger over a moody photograph of his twenty-year-old self. 'So, this was the Raphael Jordan who captured your imagination. Did I live up to your expectations in the flesh?' he teased.

'Actually, you lived down to them,' she said, straight-faced, and he laughed.

'Maybe you would have preferred me to remain your unattainable *beau ideal*?'

She put the scrapbook in the drawer. 'But this way I can have both,' she said smugly.

In a way she did have the best of both worlds, she'd consoled herself—at least for a while...that precious 'indefinite period' that Rafe had talked about.

As the ashfalls eased, replaced by a steady stream of sulphur dioxide rising from the empty crater lake to form a thin blue-brown haze above the volcanic plateau, and the weather stayed dry and cold, Paula had insisted that her daughter show Rafe some of the local sights, and so for a few hours each day they had acted like carefree tourists.

Although the three ski fields were closed to skiers, the no-go area had been reduced enough that they had been able to drive up the access road to the Whakapapa field, and then walk up to see the black scars that streaked the ash-covered snow where the rivers of mud from the crater had flooded perilously close to some of the ski lift equipment.

Jennifer had also taken Rafe on a bush walk through the native forest at the foot of Mount Tongariro, which, along with Mounts Ngaruahoe and Ruapehu, formed the rumbling threesome of active volcanoes that were the main attraction of the Tongariro National Park. Yesterday they had driven east to the Tokaanu geothermal area, where they'd strolled amongst the hissing steam vents and boiling mud pools, getting a hint of the sulphurous fury which had raged inside Ruapehu.

It had only been the suggestion of today's rafting trip that had caused Rafe to baulk.

'White water rafting?' He'd frowned dubiously as he padded after her into the kitchen, where Paula had been assembling the ingredients for breakfast. 'What if you fall out?'

'It's not very likely; the guides are very clued-up on safety. I've rafted this stretch before and no one's ever fallen out,' said Jennifer, surprised by his reluctance. She would have thought Rafe was a prime candidate for an adventurous experience.

'You weren't pregnant before,' he pointed out disapprovingly, stopping her in her tracks.

'It's only a Grade 3 river,' she explained. 'So it's not dangerous—just enough white water to get the adrenaline going, that's all. It's easy enough to be recommended everywhere as a first trip, and I've never heard of anyone being injured, so if you're nervous about being on the water—'

'I've been rafting before, and on some pretty challenging rivers—but you, of *all* people, shouldn't want to do anything that might endanger your pregnancy. How would you feel if you lost the baby because you took an unnecessary risk?'

'I'm not going to lose the baby,' she said, resenting the implication that she would be careless with her precious cargo. 'I'm pregnant, not ill, and the doctor says I'm fit, strong and healthy—I do a lot of walking with Bonzer, and lifting and stretching and heavy work around the house. I wouldn't go rafting or horseback riding in late pregnancy, but at this stage the baby's still very tiny and extremely well insulated.'

His eyes went to her trim waist. 'I just don't like the idea of you hurting yourself or our baby for the sake of entertaining me,' he said stubbornly, his lean jaw jutting.

Now *the* baby had become *our* baby. She always felt vulnerable when he chose to remind her of his claim. He had been regularly dipping into the book on childbirth he had bought, and had pestered her with his embarrassing frankness about the minute changes in her body, becoming a self-professed authority on what was good for her and expressing a compulsive interest in her determination to have a natural birth, without the aid of drugs. Much to her unease, he had also started blatantly referring to the later chapters, on early childhood development.

Paula, having one of her good days and moving quite freely without her stick, put in her gentle support of her daughter as she broke eggs into a large copper bowl and began whipping them with a large wire whisk.

'I really don't think there's any harm in it, Rafe. I have several elderly friends who've done the trip, and they said that though it was exhilarating they never felt in danger.'

So Rafe had allowed himself to be persuaded, but he had been very solicitous of Jennifer, insisting on being positioned behind her in the raft and double-checking all her safety equipment.

'I never realised you were such a worry-wart,' she had mocked softly as he tightened the buckles and straps on her life-jacket.

'I never was before,' he murmured, with a hint of grimness.

She touched the back of his hand. 'It's not such a bad thing, is it? To be worried for other people?'

He interwove his fingers with hers and lifted her hand to his mouth—a lover's salute.

'It can be if it gets out of control, and from evidence so far I suspect that you have the ability to make me thoroughly paranoid.' His smile was rueful as his mouth brushed her knuckles. 'I shudder to think what you might get up to when I'm not around.'

A shadow passed across the brightness of her day, but she banished it with a laugh as he added smokily, 'All these harnesses and straps are giving me ideas. Perhaps I should put you on a safety leash.'

'Is that one of *your* fantasies?' she teased, and her blood simmered at the look he gave her.

'Ask me that again tonight,' he growled, and tucked

his arm behind her back to guide her down to the flowing water's edge.

In the event, he had thrown himself whole-heartedly into the rafting experience, his concern for Jennifer notwithstanding, and now, after he had helped reload the rafts and they had changed back into their own clothes and handed in their wetsuits and safety gear, they decided to pick up some lunch at the tiny township of Rangipo and picnic at one of the scenic roadside spots on the way back to Beech House.

They ate their sandwiches and drank their cans of orange juice undisturbed at a weathered wooden picnic table out of sight of the road, the sunlight filtering through the high canopy of mountain beech and the lower interlacing of tree ferns to dapple on the undergrowth of fivefinger and broadleaf. It was cold, but Jennifer was well padded in her red parka and green woollen sweater, worn over jeans tucked securely into the tops of her sheepskin-lined leather boots. Rafe was wearing the same clothes in which he had arrived at Beech House, and Jennifer was awed to think how much had happened since that tumultuous day. The whole focus of her life had subtly shifted, the baby that she carried still unutterably precious and yet no longer alone in being central to her happiness.

Rafe's appetite was greater than Jennifer's, so she let him filch from her brown paper bag and laughingly fed him pieces of her crumbling custard tart. Her laughter died as he took hold of her hand and, holding her gaze, gently sucked her fingers, one by one, clean of their sweet, sticky sediment. Her breathing slowed and her body quickened, her brown eyes growing darker as she watched his lean cheeks hollow with the tugging suction, reminding her of his sultry absorption the previous night, when he had lain beside her in bed, suckling her breasts while his hand played idly between her thighs.

Still holding her hand, Rafe got to his feet, glancing around, then he was tugging her deeper into the fringes of the bush with a devilish grin, towards a towering to-tara tree whose soaring straight trunk and massive girth proclaimed more than a century's growth.

'Rafe, where are we going?' she asked breathlessly. 'We don't want to get lost…'

'We're not going far, darling, just a quick trip to para-dise…'

He swung her behind the huge totara, pushing her up against the thick, stringy bark, pulling off her knitted ski hat and plunging his hands into her soft brown hair as his mouth sealed itself over hers. She moaned, welcom-ing the familiar wet heat of his tongue, the grate of his teeth against her lips. Her arms went around him, under the heavy black leather jacket, her fingers clutching into the thick wool of his sweater as she hugged him against her, feeling her breasts flatten against his chest.

His knees pushed between hers, levering her legs apart, and he reached down between their bodies, fum-bling with the button and zip of her jeans.

'Oh, no, we can't—someone might come…' she pro-tested in delicious apprehension, but the zip parted and she heard the chink of his belt as it was hurriedly un-fastened.

'Yes—me,' he husked into her mouth, and she giggled nervously, gasping when she felt his cool hand slide into her panties, pushing them and her jeans down below the silky V of curls at the juncture of her thighs. 'Don't worry, no one will see us, and if you scream you can scream into my mouth…'

'We can't…' she moaned as he tugged at the back of her jeans and her bare bottom scraped against the matted fibres of bark. She arched against him, and with a grunt of satisfaction Rafe wrenched open the fly of his jeans and guided his thick shaft into the narrow gap between her constricted thighs, pushing himself up inside her until he felt her shudder and accept his full length in a slippery rush.

'God, I needed this...I can't ever get enough of you,' he gritted, and quickly began a tight, grinding series of jerking thrusts that he mimicked with his tongue in her mouth, his hands sliding up under her jumper to contract rhythmically on her lace-clad breasts as he brought them both to a swift, fierce convulsion of pleasure that left them weak and panting.

He pulled up her jeans and refastened their clothing as they continued to lean against the huge tree, and Jennifer slowly became aware of her surroundings beyond the warm press of his body—the muffled swish of cars out on the road, the flutter of wings and the scrape of insects, the rustle of leaves and somewhere high up in the canopy the sweet song of a white-throated tui.

'It's ironic,' he murmured, his forehead resting on hers. 'All these years I've been so very, very careful not to get any woman pregnant, not to be trapped into a relationship I didn't want. I *always* took on the responsibility for contraception every time I made love; I've always used condoms whether or not a woman said she was on the pill. And yet here I am, at thirty-three, strutting like a randy teenager at having got a girl into trouble...and finding it an incredibly erotic experience. I like not having to use any contraception with you; I like the thought of flooding more of my sperm into your fertile body; I like knowing you're lush and ripe for me because my seed is flourishing inside you...'

The first part of his speech was so shattering that Jennifer barely registered the second.

'I'm not in *trouble*,' she said tightly, looking at him through lenses which were only now clearing of the fog of their combined breath.

'Yes, you are.' He lifted his head, his eyes the same

dense, dark, concentrated green as the totara's foliage. 'You have this rosy vision of what motherhood is going to be, that once you have your baby your life is going to be complete, a charmed little circle of perfect happiness. But life isn't that neat and tidy. Motherhood is only part of being a woman. What about the rest of you? You can't live only through your child; it's not good for the child or for you. You have needs, powerful adult desires, emotional and physical, that have nothing to do with your maternal feelings. You need someone in your life who can satisfy those needs, who can give your life balance and perspective.'

His stunning words battered at her brain, filling her with such dread hope that Jennifer felt sick. She pulled out of his arms and moved over to pick up her hat, brushing off the leaves which clung to its woven surface.

'And where do I find this paragon of fulfilment?' she asked unevenly, as she turned back.

He looked away from her, his profile rigid, and for one awful instant he looked as horribly aloof as he had in London. But then he looked back, and she saw the fierce determination in his gaze as he said roughly, 'What you and I have—it's been good for both of us—I don't want it to end...'

She let out a gusty little sigh. 'Neither do I,' she admitted with grave caution, detecting the hint of resistance in his words. He didn't sound too happy about whatever it was he was going to suggest. Perhaps, like her, he was conscious of the horrendous complications involved.

But she had misjudged him, because he pounced, seizing her hands and saying eagerly, 'Then come back with me to London, Jennifer. Don't let this end here. Come and live with me and let me prove to you how happy we can be—how well we can complement each other in so many ways. As companions, lovers, partners, professional colleagues, friends...parents...' His voice deepened to urgency as he felt her fingers tense in his grasp.

'I know you were homesick last time you were there, but this time it'd be different—I'd make sure you're never lonely, and your life would be so filled to the brim with new experiences you'd never get the chance to be bored. And living with me you'd have the freedom to truly be yourself, to be able to do and be whatever you want. You could write to your heart's content until the baby's born, and then, if that's what you want, you could be a full-time mother, or let me look after our baby while you write...'

It sounded idyllic.

Come and live with me.

With Rafe, Jennifer could do and be whatever she wanted, he said...

But for one notable exception.

No matter how much she wanted it she couldn't be a *wife*.

And she had noticed that although he had spoken very passionately and persuasively, it had all been about the *practical* advantages of her going to live with him, nothing of his own feelings. Love was obviously not one of his fine inducements...

Jennifer's sickness heaved like hot lava into the back of her throat, and then died away again in a burn of acid bile.

'How long do you envisage the—arrangement—lasting?' she asked thinly.

His urgency dimmed, his eyes shuttering. 'I hadn't thought about imposing any time limit. I suppose—for as long as you were happy...naturally, I wouldn't expect you to stay with me if you were miserable,' he added stiffly.

Naturally. Just like his last 'companion'! And again,

no mention of *his* feelings. For a man who normally flaunted a painful frankness, it was a telling omission.

'What would people say about your suddenly shacking up with your pregnant stepmother?' she asked crudely, pulling her cold hands from his.

'Who cares what other people think?' he said, thrusting his empty hands into his pockets, cynical lines carving into his narrow face. 'The witches might try to give us a hard time, but I'm more than a match for anything they can dish out, and they're hardly going to rock the boat and risk tying up Sebastian's estate even longer, or alienating you as a Jordan trustee. If you're worried about gossip, don't be. London is very definitely *not* a small town, and I live a pretty private life these days—most people wouldn't even know, let alone care what you and I do together.'

He hunched his shoulders and tilted his head, striving to lighten a conversation which had somehow gone bewilderingly wrong, seeking an answering glimmer of amusement in her eyes as he said, 'Besides, as you took such convenient advantage of yourself, we have the same surname, so most people we meet as a couple will probably simply assume we're married to each other—we don't ever have to mention our convoluted family history.'

His attempt fell aggressively flat. 'So we'd live the lie over there, too. Although we wouldn't be married you'd be quite happy for people to think we were. Isn't that rather hypocritical of you?'

His eyes narrowed, his head jerking straight. 'Is *that* what this is all about, Jennifer? Marriage? You'll sleep with me for a few nights but you won't commit to me in any other way unless I ask you to marry me? What kind of twisted morality is that?'

'I never expected a marriage proposal from you. I never would,' she said proudly, the bitter truth of it blazing in her eyes. 'But the whole point of my getting married to Sebastian was to make having my baby respectable. If I moved in with you that would all be destroyed.'

'Being married is no guarantee of respectability these days.'

'It still is to my mother.'

'And your mother thinks we're married already.'

He was cutting away at her objections one by one. Soon he would be down to the quick. God, if he discovered how she felt about him he would know it was only a matter of time before he was able to wear her down. But no matter how much she was tempted, how could she make a genuine commitment to a man who didn't love her? And how could she project emotional security for her child if she didn't feel any herself?

'You said you didn't want to be *trapped* into a relationship by a pregnant woman,' she reminded him acidly.

He stepped forward and cupped her face, ignoring her stiff resistance, his thumbs smearing the bitter words from her lips as he replied with restrained ferocity. 'Damn you, I was speaking about the past. This is my *choice*, not a trap I'm stumbling blindly into. Getting to know you these last few days has meant getting to know my baby too, accepting that I don't want to back away from the excitement of nurturing a new life.' He slid his hands down to her stomach under her padded jacket. 'This baby is an intrinsic part of who you are, of who I am. How could I want you and not want the baby too? I'm not anything like Sebastian. I could be a good father if you'll give me the opportunity...'

So now he was admitting he wanted the baby. The old, foolish terror plucked at her heart: the fear of loss— now not just of her baby, but of herself.

'I belong here and so does my baby,' she said desperately, pushing herself free. 'You might have only your own selfish wants to consider, but I can't afford to just swan off and leave Mum to struggle on her own.' She turned and began to hurry back to the car.

'Why don't we ask Paula her opinion instead of you making the decision for her?'

She swung around, her hand on the door. 'No! She'd pretend it was all right for my sake. She'd just tell me what she thought I wanted to hear—'

'You mean, like you tell her what you think *she* wants to hear?' he said angrily. 'Who's the hypocrite now? Have you ever considered that maybe she'd *benefit* from being treated as a capable adult rather than as an invalid who always has to be protected? Stop using your mother as an excuse to cop out! If you're so worried about her being on her own while Dot's away, or not being able to handle the business, then let me pay for someone to move in—a sort of companion-cum-business manager. You don't have to worry about what you can *afford* any more, dammit. I'm not as rich as Sebastian but I can certainly support you and your family—'

'And that's typical of *your* family!' she cried at him, whipping herself up into a frenzy. 'Only what *you* want matters. You claim you're not like your father, but that's *exactly* the sort of thing he would have said. If you can't get something by fair and decent means, you buy it.

'Everything has a price as far as you're concerned, doesn't it, Rafe? Nothing is sacred, not even the bonds between mother and child.' She tossed her head at the murderous fury in his eyes, telling herself she didn't care. 'Well, *I* don't have a price, and you needn't think I'm going to let you buy a half-interest in my baby, either!'

The twenty-minute drive back to Beech House was achieved in blistering silence. When Rafe finally skidded to a gravelly halt on the driveway he unclipped his seat belt and wrenched open his door, before turning back to say thickly, 'Know this, Jennifer: whether you choose to have anything more to do with me or not, I expect to be registered as the father on that baby's birth certificate. I want my son or daughter to know who I am, to know that I'm proud to be a father, and that I'll welcome any child who wants to seek me out with open arms.'

'And if I don't do it, I suppose you'll threaten to sue me for custody?' she choked.

Rafe went pale. The savage heat in his gaze turned to green ice, and when he spoke it was through lips rimmed with white.

'When Sebastian knew he was never going to have any more natural children he battled my mother through the courts to try and get custody of me. When she was going through a bad patch with her second husband, and was ill, some moron of a judge, whom I've no doubt was a crony of Sebastian's, gave him temporary custody. I was nine years old and hardly knew who he was. I lived with him for six months and hated it. I was just a possession, to be bribed into silence when he was busy and expected to perform in front of his guests when he wanted to show off his heir. He didn't want me; he wanted what I symbolised. I was eventually sent back to my mother, but Sebastian kept petitioning the court for years afterwards, requesting changes in visitation rights, making her life a hell of insecurity.'

Rafe's voice actually shook as he said into Jennifer's now equally white face, 'So don't you ever, *ever* again accuse me of threatening your bond with your child. I wouldn't do that to my worst enemy, let alone the woman I love!'

She followed on trembling legs as he stormed out of the car and into the house. He slammed up the stairs to her bedroom and crashed the door shut with a resounding bang.

Paula came out of the front bedroom as Jennifer hovered in the entranceway, staring up the stairs in horror.

The woman I love?

'What's going on?' Paula saw Jennifer's face and dropped her armful of sheets. 'Jenny, darling, what's happened?'

'Oh, *Mum*!' Tears filled her eyes and Paula rushed to put her arms around her sobbing daughter, then led her into a vacant bedroom to sit on the side of the bed.

'What's wrong, darling? Is it Rafe?'

They both jumped as a crash came from upstairs, then a pounding clatter on the stairs and the front door slamming. Looking out of the window, they could see Rafe striding full-tilt across the lawn towards the far trees, Bonzer panting at his heels, his hands thrust into the pockets of his leather jacket, his body leaning into the wind as if welcoming the slicing chill.

'What is it, Jen? Have you had an argument?'

Jennifer stared at her mother's thin, anxious face in an agony of indecision. Her mind tracked into a future where *her* child was an adult, and suddenly there was no decision to make. It all became obvious. And there was an obvious place to start. To offer her faith in the future. She jumped to her feet, scrubbing her cheeks under her glasses.

'Just a moment. I have to get something to show you.' She ran upstairs and pulled one of her books out of the bookcase, the one with the raunchiest cover.

Back in the bedroom, her mother was still sitting patiently where she had left her, and Jennifer silently handed her the slim volume, mentally bracing herself.

'What's this?' Her mother blinked a little as she saw the cover.

'I wrote it,' Jennifer said baldly, and her mother's brow wrinkled.

'But it says Lacey Graham—'

'I know, that's the pen-name I use. I've had nine books published by Rafe's company—he's my editor. I've been writing them for years.'

Paula looked bewildered and began to open the book, and Jennifer hurriedly put her hand on it.

'They're—there's a lot of sex in them, Mum. They're erotic books for women. That's why I never told you about them. I— I make quite a bit of money on them.' She named the sum of her last royalties, which made her mother's eyes widen.

'Goodness, you must be quite good at it.'

Jennifer smiled a watery smile. 'Very good, actually. Rafe said he thought you should be proud of me.'

'Then so I shall be,' her mother said stoutly. 'Is that why you and Rafe quarrelled? Because he wanted to tell me and you were embarrassed?'

'I thought *you'd* be embarrassed.'

'Well, I suppose I might be, darling, when I get around to reading one,' her mother said, going a little pink. 'But sex is a natural part of life after all. I think I'll still want to boast about my daughter the author— except to the vicar, of course!'

'Oh, Mum!' Jennifer shook her head helplessly— she'd been so wrong about so very many things. And such a coward. She'd taken Rafe's words at face value without looking for the meaning beneath the surface, without realising that Rafe, too, was fiercely self-protective. A man so cautious of marriage would be even more cautious of love, of declaring and of accepting it in return. It had been a huge step for him just to admit that he had changed his attitude about children, and the woman he loved had thrown it back in his face!

'Rafe and I didn't quarrel about that—not exactly.' She hugged her arms around her waist. 'He wants me to go back to England with him and I was worried about leaving you.'

'Well, I didn't expect him to move in here with us, Jen,' her mother said deflatingly. 'Of *course* your place is with your husband. How could it be otherwise? You never talked about it, but I knew that after his Amazon trip was over you would fly the nest with Rafe—I thought that was why you were arranging all those medical benefits for me. I guessed when Rafe mentioned about how we could use the upstairs room as a suite that it wouldn't be long before you were leaving. It's a good idea of his about the room, don't you think? You wouldn't mind us turning it into a guestroom? Of course, we'd make sure it was kept free for when you and Rafe and the baby visit...'

Paula was full of plans, and so, suddenly, was Jennifer. Why had she insisted on making life so complicated for herself when it was really all so blindingly simple? Rafe was right—they *could* work things out, providing that she *wanted* to work things out. And she knew now that she did, that she wanted to embrace life, not hide from it or live it only vicariously, through her books.

She ran across the waving grass, listening for Bonzer's bark but hearing only the empty wind in the beech trees along the drive. Through the shrubbery around the back of the cottage garden she thought she saw a glimpse of Bonzer's waving tail, and she veered towards the orchard in so much haste she almost missed him.

Rafe was leaning against the side of Dot's ramshackle potting shed, his head tilted back against the weathered timber, his eyes closed, and as she stepped closer on the soft earth she could see a faint glister on the high cheekbones and a thin trail of silver through the stubble on the side of his jaw.

Oh, God...

The shock of fierce tenderness that pierced Jennifer's

heart nearly sent her to her knees. He had freely displayed his rage but he had come out here to hide like a little boy with his pain, like the lonely, bewildered nine-year-old boy he must have been in his father's house, desperately missing his mother and struggling against a deep sense of emotional isolation.

'Rafe…'

Her soft sigh made his eyelids flicker in alarm, but they merely closed tighter, and he quickly raised his forearm to rest across his eyes, his fist clenched.

Not just pain—but grief and anger. She moved around in front of him, knowing that the measure of his hurt was also a measure of his love. He might never be able to bring himself to say it to her again, but she would know…

'Rafe, darling…please, look at me.'

He didn't move, his body a rigid line of fierce rejection, and she put her tentative hands on his chest, feeling the sharp recoil of his muscles.

She picked up his balled fist from his side and pressed her lips to the white knuckles, then placed it between her breasts against her heart, wondering how to begin. It awed and shamed her to think that she had brought the man she loved to the point of tears.

'I'm so afraid of you,' she whispered. 'So awfully afraid of what you make me feel. You make me feel so greedy and needy—wanting things that I thought I could never have.' She pressed herself against the rigid wall of his body, trapping his hand between them, resting her cheek against his chest, absorbing the shuddering beat of his heart as she slid her arms around his lean waist, knowing that she was going to have to humble herself and not caring.

'Like you…I never thought I would be able to have you, except for this one, brief time. I couldn't let myself even think of what a future with you would be like. I couldn't even admit to myself that I loved you, let alone admit it to you. I was afraid it would give you too much power to hurt me...'

He didn't move, but the quality of his rigidity had changed, his tension now charged with a new stillness.

'I want— I want to be with you. I want to be allowed to love you, I want to *be* loved. I want to give you our child to love and be loved. I want you to have everything that you want and be happy for ever, and if I can give you any small part of that happiness I will.' She buried her face in his chest. 'So, please, ask me again, Rafe...ask me to come and live with you and be your love and prove all the pleasures with you. Or, if you won't—let *me* do the asking...'

The arm that was over his eyes came down over her head, across the back of her shoulders, the fist still clenched.

'Damn you! How could you do that to me?' he said rawly, his angry breath stirring her fringe, and she knew it was going to be all right. 'How could you listen to me tell you I love you and want to live my life with you, and turn me away like that, with those words?'

She lifted her head against the brace of his arm, letting him see her drenched brown eyes, seeing the bloodshot green of his. 'But you didn't tell me you loved me,' she said gently. 'You didn't say anything about love until just now, in the car.'

'I must have—I told you I wanted you, and my baby, and you kicked me in the teeth.'

'I'm sorry.' She lifted her hand and laid it along his rough cheek, her thumb stroking his jaw, feeling the dampness there. 'But I didn't know how you felt, only what *I* was feeling. I was so confused and it just sounded as if you wanted things convenient for *you*.'

'I've never told a woman I loved her before,' he said fiercely. 'I was working up to it slowly, and you jumped in and wanted to know how long it would last, as if you thought you'd get tired of me.'

Tired of *Rafe*? She looked into his grim expression and knew that they had been racked by the same uncertainties.

'I'm sorry,' she said again, meekly. 'Did I ruin your big declaration?'

Colour came into his pale face and his arms slid down around her waist, and suddenly the rich humour was back in his eyes. 'Yes, you did. So I guess I'll have to do it all over again. Jennifer, darling…?'

'Yes, Rafe?'

He smiled warmly. 'Will you come to London and marry me and have more of my babies?'

She almost slid through the bracelet of his arms, and her stomach swooped, but her love sustained her to accept his teasing.

'Rafe, I've said I'm sorry. I understand why you feel the way you do about marriage,' she said quietly. 'You once asked me to see you as *you*—well, I do. And it's *you* I love. The way you are…' She smiled back mischieviously. 'Hang-ups and all. As long as I know you love me too. I don't need the piece of paper—'

'But maybe *I* need it,' he said. 'It gave me a shock to realise how possessive I felt about you and the baby, how outraged at the thought of not being allowed to be part of your life. I'm *not* going to let my father's mistakes rule my life and manipulate my thinking. I have nothing to prove any more—except my love to you.'

She put her finger across his warm lips. 'You don't have to prove anything, or to bribe me with a wedding ring. I respect your word, Rafe, whatever promise you give me is enough.'

He nipped her finger. 'Then I promise I'll love you for the rest of my life; I promise I'll never be unfaithful to you; I promise I'll never leave you; I promise I'll never abuse your trust or lie to you, or our children; I promise to cherish and protect you and even, on occasions, to obey.'

She shook her head, tears of love pricking her eyes. 'And how do you know you can keep them all?'

'Because now I have something I've lacked all these years. Faith. You've given that to me, Jennifer. Faith in my own character—faith to know when the right woman finally comes along—faith in my love for my woman and hers for me—faith in the life and the future we can create together.'

She linked her arms around his neck, going on tiptoe to touch her mouth to his in loving homage and enjoying his heady response. 'Who would have thought when Sebastian arranged for me to have my baby that this would happen?' she sighed.

'Who indeed?' he murmured, so drily that she tilted her face up with a frown.

'What?' She saw the answer in his face and her jaw dropped. 'You think he *planned* for this to happen?'

'Well, I don't know about *this* exactly.' He nudged her with his hips, enjoying her sudden flush. 'But he certainly did his best to get us entangled in as many ways as he could after he was gone, didn't he? Maybe he hoped propinquity and nature would do the rest.'

Jennifer glanced over her shoulder at the mountain, smouldering quietly against a hazy blue sky. 'Well, nature certainly played its part.' She dimpled.

'But propinquity was the best bit,' he said, kissing her to prove it.

'What are we going to tell my mother?' she wondered ruefully when she surfaced.

He grinned. 'Nothing. She's happy we're husband and wife, so let's leave it that way—unless you want a big, flashy wedding?' He laughed when Jennifer shook her head frantically; she just wanted their lives together to start as quickly and smoothly and quietly as possible. 'Maybe after we give her a third grandchild we might start dropping hints about the secret of our romantic past,' he suggested.

'Romantic!' Jennifer rolled her eyes. 'You mean tormented and torrid!'

'That too. Speaking of which...' He scooped her up in his arms and began to carry her back to the house, looking down at her with the light of love and laughter in his eyes.

'Well, Mrs Jordan, I think that after we turn our pretend marriage into the real thing we'll have earned ourselves a *real* honeymoon. And I've got the perfect place for it...'

'Oh?' She heard the innocent note in his voice, and laughter was bubbling up from her throat even before he finished speaking.

'Yes—I know this fantastic little remote and isolated spot on the banks of the mighty Amazon...!'

Take 2 bestselling love stories FREE

Plus get a FREE surprise gift!

Special Limited-Time Offer

Mail to Harlequin Reader Service®

3010 Walden Avenue
P.O. Box 1867
Buffalo, N.Y. 14240-1867

YES! Please send me 2 free Harlequin Presents® novels and my free surprise gift. Then send me 6 brand-new novels every month, which I will receive months before they appear in bookstores. Bill me at the low price of $3.12 each plus 25¢ delivery and applicable sales tax, if any*. That's the complete price, and a saving of over 10% off the cover prices—quite a bargain! I understand that accepting the books and gift places me under no obligation ever to buy any books. I can always return a shipment and cancel at any time. Even if I never buy another book from Harlequin, the 2 free books and the surprise gift are mine to keep forever.

106 HEN CH69

Name	(PLEASE PRINT)

Address	Apt. No.

City	State	Zip

This offer is limited to one order per household and not valid to present Harlequin Presents® subscribers. *Terms and prices are subject to change without notice. Sales tax applicable in N.Y.

UPRES-98 ©1990 Harlequin Enterprises Limited

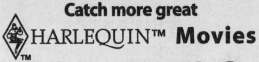 

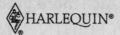

Not The Same Old Story!

 Exciting, glamorous romance stories that take readers around the world.

Harlequin Romance® Sparkling, fresh and tender love stories that bring you pure romance.

HARLEQUIN® *Temptation* Bold and adventurous— Temptation is strong women, bad boys, great sex!

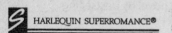 Provocative and realistic stories that celebrate life and love.

 Contemporary fairy tales—where anything is possible and where dreams come true.

HARLEQUIN® **INTRIGUE**® Heart-stopping, suspenseful adventures that combine the best of romance and mystery.

LOVE & LAUGHTER™ Humorous and romantic stories that capture the lighter side of love.

Mysterious, sexy, sizzling...

THE AUSTRALIANS

Stories of romance Australian-style, guaranteed to
fulfill that sense of adventure!

This November look for

Borrowed—One Bride

by **Trisha David**

Beth Lister is surprised when Kell Hallam kidnaps her on her
wedding day and takes her to his dusty ranch, Coolbuma. Just
who is Kell, and what is his mysterious plan? But Beth is even
more surprised when passion begins to rise between her and
her captor!

*The Wonder from Down Under: where spirited women win
the hearts of Australia's most independent men!*

Available November 1998
where books are sold.

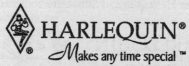

HARLEQUIN®
Makes any time special ™

**SEXY, POWERFUL MEN NEED
EXTRAORDINARY WOMEN WHEN THEY'RE**

*Destined
for
Love*

Take a walk on the wild side this October
when three bestselling authors weave wondrous stories
about heroines who use their extraspecial abilities to
achieve the magic and wonder of love!

HATFIELD AND McCOY
by HEATHER GRAHAM POZZESSERE

LIGHTNING STRIKES
by KATHLEEN KORBEL

MYSTERY LOVER
by ANNETTE BROADRICK

Available October 1998
wherever Harlequin and Silhouette books are sold.

HARLEQUIN®
Makes any time special ™

Silhouette®